WHAT HAPPENS AT CON

Cathy Yardley

Copyright © 2018 by Cathy Wilson

All rights reserved.

No portion of this book may be reproduced in any form without written permission from the publisher or author, except as permitted by U.S. copyright law.

Contents

1. CHAPTER 1 — 1
2. CHAPTER 2 — 27
3. CHAPTER 3 — 49
4. CHAPTER 4 — 71
5. CHAPTER 5 — 97
6. CHAPTER 6 — 117
7. CHAPTER 7 — 140
8. CHAPTER 8 — 159
9. CHAPTER 9 — 178
10. CHAPTER 10 — 195
11. CHAPTER 11 — 210
12. CHAPTER 12 — 223
13. EPILOGUE — 230

A Note From Cathy	234
About Author	236
Let's Get Social	237
Also By	238

CHAPTER 1

Ani Choudhary took a deep breath, hurrying across the grassy quad, her cell phone to her ear. "You didn't have to call me," she said, trying not to sound out of breath.

"It's my fault that you have to meet your new adviser, just a month or two before your proposal defense," Dr. Delilah Kantor said. "I just feel bad."

"It's not your fault you got breast cancer," Ani said, trying to sound reassuring. "You need to rest up, take care of yourself."

"I should be able to take you on after I get through with all this," Delilah said, but her voice did sound tired. "Anyway, Dr. Peterson is one of the best in immunology at the Maple Valley campus."

Ani sighed quietly. "I'm sure he'll be great," she said, not so much lying as trying to be optimistic. She knew he had a great reputation. It was why she'd gone with him. But rumor had it Dr. Peterson was old-school. He was very set in his ways, in his methods. In his beliefs.

He also had very few women on his research teams, and he advised very few of them. That, she worried, was going to be a problem.

"All right. I'm here," Ani said as she arrived at the office. "Take care of yourself, and I'll visit soon, okay?"

"Ani, you're going to be working on your proposal defense and doing your RA work. You'll barely have time to bathe," Delilah said with a weak laugh. "Don't worry about me, all right? I've got Richard here. I'm fine."

Richard was Delilah's husband, and a registered surgical nurse. Delilah would be fine, Ani knew. Or at least as fine as she could be, considering. "Well, hang in there," Ani said, feeling at a loss.

"You, too."

Ani hung up, then squared her shoulders. She had a lot riding on this. Dr. Peterson was supposed to help carry her through her proposal, the last time a student could really fail before working towards her PhD. That didn't mean she wasn't going to be working her ass off for a couple of years after the proposal defense — it just meant that if they wanted to get rid of her, her advisory board would probably choose that time to do so, rather than have her go through all the work of a dissertation and pull together the entire board at the same time just to fail her. She'd already worked over the project concept with Delilah ad nauseum over the past two years while she finished her generals and got all the foundations of her career. She'd then gone off to Helsinki for nearly a year, at Delilah's request. She trusted Ani to do the research and capture the information necessary.

She could've chosen Dr. Peterson when she'd first applied to Washington Sound University, but Delilah was another woman in the field, and Ani knew that Delilah would understand the difficulties better. Also, Delilah's research team was a good mix of men and women who were diverse as well as solid researchers and students.

When Ani stepped in, the research team was just assembling. "Ready to meet him?" her friend Linda said with a smile. Linda was a transplant from Delilah's research team, as well. "I've heard he used to be a Marine or something. He's supposed to be like Atilla the Hun."

"Oh?" Ani had heard that, too, but she didn't want to confirm or deny anything — she didn't want to influence Linda, not yet. Still, she felt her stomach knot. "What specifically makes you say that? What have you heard?"

"Not a lot I can confirm, but stuff that makes me worry. You with your specifics," Linda teased, but Ani heard the nerves behind it.

"We're grad students. And lab researchers," Ani said, nudging her. "We're *supposed* to be all about specifics."

Linda's voice dropped. "I heard he's only had one other woman on his research team. She wore a miniskirt to the lab, and he brought her into his office and talked to her. She left crying."

"What the hell?" Ani's eyes widened, and her fists balled. "Did he... He didn't..."

Linda caught on. "No, he didn't touch her. From what I heard, he just told her that—"

The door opened, and Linda's mouth snapped shut. Dr. Peterson was tall, and he looked like Josh Brolin's father... the guy who was married to Barbara Streisand, all salt-and-pepper dignified, with broad shoulders. He looked like a military guy, ramrod straight. Maybe because of the stick up his ass, Ani thought, then struggled to choke back a nervous laugh.

She shouldn't be so judgmental. Maybe the rumors were just that, rumors. She knew better than anyone not to judge by appearances.

Another man, shorter, with sunshine-gold hair and sort of Abercrombie and Fitch good looks, trailed in Dr. Peterson's wake. He was carrying a notebook and looked eager, like a puppy. Dr. Peterson's puppy. That must be one of his teaching assistants, Ani thought. Linda had been one of Delilah's TAs, and she wondered if she'd transfer to Dr. Peterson's team. Ani was lucky enough to have joined on as one of Dr. Peterson's RAs — research assistants — so she still got a stipend.

Although given the crying woman rumor, *lucky* might be a slight misnomer.

"I've agreed to be your adviser while Dr. Kantor is indisposed," he said without preamble, all business. "You're going to notice that I run the lab a bit differently than Dr.

Kantor. What are the two traits I value above all in my research team, Jeffrey?"

Golden Retriever Boy — Jeffrey, apparently — spoke up. "Rigor and repetition, sir."

Sir? Delilah had been fine with being called by her first name.

Dr. Peterson nodded. "You need both if you're going to achieve your doctorate. Some of you have proposal defenses coming up..."

Ani swallowed hard. He wasn't really looking at her, though.

"If that's the case, I'm going to make sure you reach a level of competence that perhaps you wouldn't have otherwise."

"Dr. Kantor upheld high standards of competence," Ani blurted out, feeling offended, both for her own sake and the sake of her mentor.

He turned on her like a velociraptor, as if he'd deliberately baited the team to get just such a reaction. "Aha! What's your name, miss...?"

"Choudhary. Ani Choudhary," Ani replied.

"I take it you've got a proposal defense scheduled soon?" he said, shaking his head. "I hope you're not too sensitive. We're not like the humanities, Miss Ani. We're more about the data than feelings, so I hope you realize that we can often be more brusque in our manners of speech."

And apparently condescending, she thought, but held her tongue.

"Meet me in my office after this," he said, and she felt her stomach drop. "Oh, and I wanted to tell you that Jeffrey here is my TA and another grad student I am advising. He will be joining your research team. If you have questions, please run them through him... odds are better that he can help you with smaller-level details. I hate being bothered by minutiae." He turned, heading toward his office, then looked over his shoulder. "All right. Get on with your work. And Miss Ani, please follow me."

Ani did as instructed after shooting Linda a quick, worried glance. Linda looked apologetic. She walked into the man's office. It wasn't much to look at, but some of the knickknacks looked expensive, as did his clothes. She got the feeling he came from money, even if he was no-nonsense about it. He probably wasn't snobbish that way.

"What are you studying, Miss Ani?"

She wondered what his reasons were for calling her Miss Ani. She thought about correcting him to Ms., but again, it seemed like the wrong time. The fact that he called her Ani, her first name, rather than her last, put her at a slight disadvantage — she called him his last name, or "sir" if she followed Jeffrey's example, and now she was supposed to answer to her first name?

Subtle power imbalance. *Gah*.

"Is focusing is a difficulty for you?" he said when she didn't answer immediately.

"I just wanted to make sure I was answering as clearly as possible," she said quietly, playing for demure. "Rigor, as you say."

He raised an eyebrow. "We'll see," she heard him mutter.

She felt the room squeeze her. "I'm studying immunology…"

"Obviously," he said. "That's the best you can do? That took five minutes to come up with?"

She gritted her teeth. "Specifically, I'm studying—"

"In a nutshell. I'm not here to listen to your dissertation proposal." He frowned. "At least, not for some weeks, if I remember correctly."

Deep breath, Ani. "I'm studying natural killer cells — their activation and contribution to—"

"Huh. Saw that done before," he said, and it was all she could do not to jump over the desk and throttle him. "You're really going to need to impress with this proposal. You want to get your doctorate, don't you?"

"*Yes*." When she saw that he seemed to be waiting impatiently, she added, "Sir."

"This is a difficult pursuit," he said, his light blue eyes looking unnatural — and off-putting. "I don't have time for hand-holding, and I'm not interested in listening to excuses. You're going to have to do this largely on your own, and you're going to need to do it perfectly. I don't coddle my mentees."

And thank God for that. Any more time in his cheerful company and she'd be wanted for murder.

"And I'm not interested in dealing with sulking or crying, so don't try it," he warned. "You wouldn't be the first, and I've got no patience for it."

Could he be any more insulting?

"That said, if you can survive the program, if you get through your proposal defense, it would have the imprimatur of quality on it. I'm known as a tough professor for a reason, Miss Ani," he said, his voice just this side of sharp. "I expect students to pull their weight and prove to me that they deserve the doctorate."

"I have six weeks left until my proposal defense," she said. "Most of the work I did with Dr. Kantor, under her express supervision. I feel that I'm ready—"

"But it doesn't matter if you think you're ready, does it?" he cut in. "If you don't meet *my* standards at the proposal defense, then you're done, do you understand? I don't care what your previous adviser told you. From now on, you're my student, my research assistant, and one of my teaching assistants. I expect you to produce a worthwhile presentation. And I expect that you're able to maintain the standards and fulfil the duties I outline for all my TAs and RAs. Got it?"

She blinked. TA? That was news to her, but she'd admit she could use the extra money... if she could carve out the time. She nodded.

He looked at her, tilting his head a little, staring at her. "Do you, really?" he said. "Say it like you mean it, please."

"Yes. Sir," she added, with just the slightest bit of sarcasm. Which was a Herculean effort, she had to say.

His damned eyebrow quirked up again. "We'll just see how this goes," he said, and his tone was dark with foreboding.

She left the office, her blood on a solid boil. Her new adviser was an asshole, no question. And she got the feeling when she showed up for her duties as his TA and RA on Monday, he'd be scrutinizing her every breath.

She got in her car, and headed for Snoqualmie,, and the Frost Fandoms bookstore. Because after a day like today, what she really needed was her best friends and a multitude of drinks, in that order. With luck, they were both in the same place.

Video game night should've been a lot more relaxing, Abraham Williams thought with a growl. It used to be a lot more relaxing, anyway. But tonight, it was turning into just a pain in the ass.

"What's going on with you, Abraham?" Jose asked when Abraham got killed and let out a blue streak of cursing.

"Other than I fucking hate losing?"

"Well, obviously," his other friend Fezza noted, his slim shoulders shrugging. "But you seem edgy, boss."

Even though both Jose and Fezza technically worked for him — he was their supervisor at Mysterious Pickle Games, or MPG — they were still his friends. While some would think that a boss-subordinate relationship shouldn't work, it did in their weird case, probably because they spent a lot of time together, especially when they were under stressful deadlines. Also, the guys were bonded through their mutual love of video games, movies, and assorted geekery.

Besides, if anybody got disrespectful at work, he'd shut them down. If they got disrespectful outside of work, there was a good chance he'd knock them out.

Tonight, though, his discontent wasn't a matter of disrespect, so he couldn't yell at anybody or hit anybody.

It was just that everybody else was so... so...

God. Damned. Happy.

"Tessa's going out tonight," Adam, a producer at MPG and host of tonight's game night, said with a small smile. "Headed over to the bookstore."

"Oooh, the bookstore," Jose said, his eyebrows wiggling. "Hell, why don't we head on over there too? All those sisters. Is Rachel going to be home?"

"Don't be a dick about my girlfriend's friends," Adam said absently. Jose's horndog comments and behaviors were so ingrained they were largely ignored. "Besides, tonight it's girls only. Sounds like her friend Ani is having a tough time, so they're doing some secret female rituals to help her feel better."

"Like what? Witchcraft?" Fezza asked, genuinely curious.

"If by witchcraft you mean watching *Practical Magic* and getting drunk on lime margaritas, then yes, I imagine some sort of sorcery is involved," Adam replied.

Abraham could feel the scowl on his face. "Damn it. Tessa's one of the best Overwatch players we have," he said, feeling petty but still disregarding it. "I wanted her on my team."

Dennis, one of the new guys at the company, scoffed. "Hey, I'm good. I'll play on your team, help you kick some ass." He'd only been working at MPG for a few weeks, but he seemed to fit into the culture like a Lego piece, snapping right in. He was also ex-army, something that Abraham appreciated. He hadn't met a lot of military guys in game development. Dennis was young, like twenty-three, and he was still relatively low-level. Still, he seemed to like being there.

"I still like having Tessa on my team," Abraham groused.

"You didn't want her on your team less than a year ago," Adam said, his voice a little tight.

Adam was having a hard time letting that one go, probably because Tessa was his girlfriend. "I didn't want her on my software design team," he said, staring Adam down. "It was different, and you know it. And she's more than proven herself. I wouldn't trust her with her own game now otherwise."

Tessa had impressed the hell out of him, with her coding and her initiative. Recently, she'd come up with a small game on her own, using the engine she'd been building in her spare time before she'd gotten the promotion. He'd given her the okay to run with it. Which meant she was going to be under the gun with the team for the next few months while he advised her. It was going to be interesting, standing back and handing off the reins for a bit.

"She deserves the chance," Adam said, nodding with satisfaction. "I'm glad you're giving it to her."

"Yeah, well, let's see how much you thank me when she's pushing sixty- to eighty-hour weeks in the final stretch," Abraham said.

"And when all your laundry is dirty, and you have no food in the house," Dennis added with a laugh.

"What is this, the fifties?" Adam said, rolling his eyes. "I help when I can. We take turns with household chores. And when she was sick, I made food for her."

"You are so pussy-whipped," Dennis said, and Abraham laughed.

The door swung open. "Good God, I've stepped back in time," a British voice drawled. "To think, I used to spend every waking hour with you lot."

Abraham arched an eyebrow at the Rodney, who had just stepped in. "Another whipped one," he said. "Your girlfriend know where you are? Did you escape out a window or something?"

"I just dropped Stacy off at the bookstore," he said. "And I'd rather be whipped by that beautiful woman than scowling and flogging my own rod, if you get my meaning."

The remark set off a bunch of laughter from the other guys. Abraham clenched his jaw. The guy might have a point. It'd been a while since he'd hooked up with someone. The women he met at bars or clubs... well, there was often a sheen of desperation there. Either an eager hopefulness — "maybe this guy will be The One!" — or a bedraggled hopelessness, as if they knew there was no way he could be, but they had to go through the motions on the off chance, or because they had nothing better to do.

It was... uncomfortable. Demoralizing.

"I'll be honest," Adam said, clearing his throat, "I'm gonna ask Tessa to marry me."

The rest of the guys stopped and stared at him.

"Are you fucking nuts?" Abraham snapped. "You guys have only been going together... what, six months?"

"But we lived together a year before that," Adam said.

"As roommates!"

"I've known her even longer," Adam continued stubbornly.

"But... but..." Abraham shook his head, looking at Fezza and Jose for help. They shrugged. "Seriously. Why?"

"Because I love her, dude. I don't wanna wait anymore."

"Congrats, man," Fezza said with a broad smile before turning back to the controller. "That's awesome. It's cool to see you two so happy."

Happy. That again. Abraham tried not to scowl. He probably failed miserably.

"So, I've really got no chance with her now, huh?" Jose joked, and Adam smacked him on the back of the head.

"Damn it. I'm thinking the same with Stacy, but she's got trust issues," Rodney said. "I figure I'll give her another year, but being honest, I'll be lucky to make it six months."

"Maybe you can have a long engagement," Fezza suggested. He tended to be the team problem solver.

"Jesus, could we *not* talk about weddings and engagements and shit?" Abraham snapped. "Or do we have to finally turn in our man cards? Not all of us have our balls tucked away in our girlfriends' purses!"

Abraham knew that he was being an asshole. He was known to be surly, and generally he didn't care, but this was... These guys were his friends. This was good news. He didn't have to be so shitty.

"Sorry. Congrats, all that. I am... *happy* for you." He took a deep breath. In a weird way, he was, sort of. He *wanted* his friends to be happy. But his own corresponding emotion was an empty, gnawing sort of feeling, a hollow echo of their happiness. "My parents are on my shit to get married. Just put up with an hour-long conversation with my mom the other day about why I don't have a girlfriend, blah blah. Sick of those conversations."

Sick of being alone all the time. That thought was the most galling of all.

Jose sighed. "Oh, yeah. That sucks."

"She keeps asking me when I'm gonna bring somebody by," Abraham said.

"Dude, does she know you at all?" Fezza joked, firing up a new game. "I don't think you've dated in the entire time I've known you, and I've been at MPG for, like, four years."

"I've had a girlfriend. Girlfriends," he corrected. Not for several years, admittedly, and the bulk of them were in high school before he shipped out. Like Becky... he shook his head. He wasn't going to think about that whole train wreck. He turned his attention back to the screen, choosing his character, jumping from one ledge to the next. "Focus on the game, guys. I'm done talking about this."

"Maybe the girls at the bookstore can fix you up," Rodney said, ignoring his statement.

"How come they never volunteer to fix me up?" Jose asked. They laughed.

"Fix up the horndog? Are you kidding?"

"Maybe you just need to get laid," Dennis said to Abraham, with that smug tone that reminded him of his bros when he was in the army. "Unless you've got a problem in that department, too, huh buddy?"

The room went quiet, and Abraham looked away from the screen to glare at him. Dennis was pretty mouthy — it was bravado, he felt sure. Abraham glared at him, and Dennis backed down, as Abraham thought he would, obviously sensing that his teasing had crossed a line. They weren't that close friends, not yet anyway. The fact that Abraham was six foot three and still worked out like he was in the army didn't hurt when it came to intimidation.

"What do you think?" Abraham asked, watching as Dennis's throat bobbed with a visible swallow. "Think I've got problems hooking up when I want to?"

Dennis laughed weakly. "I was just gonna suggest a bet."

Now everybody perked up. If there was one thing the MPG crew enjoyed, it was a good bet.

"For all of us non-pussy-whipped single guys," Dennis said, trying to get the vibe back with a chuckle, "we see who can hook up first."

"No contest," Jose said. "My Tinder-Fu is legendary."

"Nope! Not Tinder, not online dating, not anybody you've hooked up with before," Dennis said with a small smirk.

Fezza looked baffled. "So — old-school? Hit on somebody at a club or bar or something?"

"Sort of. A special event," Dennis said. "Erotic City Con."

"A con?" Fezza perked up. He loved conventions of all types.

"The crème de la crème of freaks are gonna be there," Dennis said, excited. "If we all hit it... we'll all *hit it*, if you know what I mean." Given his leer, it was impossible to miss the implication.

Abraham frowned. "Are we talking like..."

"Like bondage and stuff!" Dennis said. "And chicks wearing next to nothing. Lots of costumes. And, I dunno, public sex scenes and shit. It'll be *insane*."

"I'm in," Jose said.

"Um... I guess?" Fezza said.

Abraham could feel their stares on him, but he refused to buckle, focusing on the game. "What are the stakes? Of the bet?" he said instead, his character slicing and dicing its way through enemy robots.

He could hear the tones of satisfaction in Dennis's voice. "Besides bragging rights? Good point. Maybe a hundred bucks each, to make it interesting?"

Abraham shook his head. "Our stakes are never money."

"They're usually shame," Jose interjected helpfully.

"Like dressing up like Sailor Moon," Adam added, and Abraham could hear the smile in his voice.

"So — last one to hook up has to dress like... what, bikini Leia?"

"On second thought, I'm out," Fezza said. "I never hook up at cons."

"Or much of anywhere," Jose said, and Fezza threw some popcorn at him.

While Adam yelled at them to clean up their mess, Abraham shook his head. "I'm not into this bet, either. Sorry."

"Why not?" Dennis pressed.

"Too easy," Abraham said, because he didn't want to say the real reason: he felt weird about it. He usually didn't have trouble finding a woman willing to grind with him, to just hit it with no strings. But he'd found himself more and more picky lately and feeling pressured because of winning a bet left a bad taste in his mouth. "And no stakes."

"Maybe we could make a bet to get you to go?" Dennis said.

Abraham looked at the kid. Dennis seemed really eager to go to this scene. He wondered what the story was there. It might be because Dennis was new, and didn't have many friends in this area. He'd moved to Seattle to work in the gaming industry, and he'd latched onto all of them.

"What kind of bet?"

"Drink off," Dennis said, with a smile. "I brought some apple pie moonshine. If you don't stay standing, you have to go to Erotic City."

"Oh, no," Fezza said, looking green just at the mention of it.

"Um, I'm in," Jose said.

"Hand over keys and give me phone passcodes. I'm getting Ubers for your dumb asses if you go through with this," Adam said sharply.

Abraham thought about it. If there was one thing he knew how to do, it was hold his booze. His father had taught him, and the military had only reinforced it when he was on leave. "What the hell," he said. "Pour me some."

It helped fill the emptiness, if nothing else. Besides, he had a higher tolerance than most people he knew. What was the worst that could happen?

"I need a drink," Ani said to her best friend, Tessa.

They were at a bookstore, which wasn't the normal place you'd think about having a drink, but this wasn't just any bookstore. Technically, it was a collectibles and bookstore, for one thing. For another, it was currently closed as the owners and some select friends let the booze flow. Finally, those owners were the Frost sisters, friends that Tessa had made in the past year. They were awesome, and Ani felt lucky to be friends with them by association. Ani was more outgoing and less socially awkward than Tessa — of course, a potato was less socially awkward than Tessa, sometimes, much as Ani loved her — but this was like a crazy band of supportive, amazing girlfriends. She'd had that support in Tessa, but having a whole group was a new experience for her, and she valued it.

For a woman going into a STEM career with a new sexist asshat adviser, heading into her proposal defense, a group of girlfriends at her back was exactly what she needed.

"Better make that a slew of drinks," Ani corrected.

"Lime margaritas are on the way," Rachel assured her. Rachel was the oldest of the Frost sisters, and an absolute stunner. Ani wasn't quite sure what the story on Rachel was, besides the fact that she worked her ass off. She was the only one of the sisters who didn't solely work at the bookstore: she had an event planning job up at the casino, and then she was also going for her MBA at the University of Washington. Ani had considered going back to U Dub for her doctorate, but the smaller Washington Sound College, over in Maple Valley, had its own cache, and had presented an excellent scholarship package and attracted a lot of heavy-hitting scholars in her field.

Hailey, the middle sister, walked up with a frost margarita, rimmed in salt. "Man trouble?" she asked. Her hair was pinned up in victory rolls, and she wore a red-and-white halter top with jean shorts. She looked like a pin-up Rosie the Riveter. She was tougher than Rachel, her hair browner than Rachel's glossy black.

"Kind of man trouble," Ani said, sipping the margarita and forcing herself not to cough. Had any lime gotten into this thing, or was it pure tequila? "Um, my original adviser at school got sick — breast cancer — so someone else is taking over for her. That someone else seems to be an assbag. He's got a huge ego, likes to be called sir, doesn't think that my old adviser had enough smarts or rigor, warned me that I have to really step up my game and impress him… that kind of thing. "

"I hate guys like that," Hailey growled. Rachel nodded in dark agreement.

"Anyway, after giving me a reverse pep talk about how hard it was all going to be, I came here, seeking to drown my sorrows." She lifted her glass. "And you guys are the best friends I could've lifted a glass with, so thanks for that."

"She's getting sentimental on us," Hailey teased. Tessa laughed. It was nice to see her shy friend breaking out of her shell.

"I'm surprised you're here with us, actually, Tessa," Hailey said. "Thought you were over playing the big video game thing with Adam and the guys tonight."

"My girl needed me," Tessa said simply, making Ani feel both guilty and special.

"I didn't want you to cancel things for me!"

Tessa rolled her eyes. "Adam and Abraham can manage to kick some Overwatch ass without me for one night," she said, then frowned. "Besides, Dennis's there. I don't really get along with him so much."

"Probably for the best," Ani agreed, then sighed. "It'll get better. I just have six weeks or so before the proposal. I can put up with nearly anything for six weeks, right?"

"What kind of proposal?" Rachel asked.

"It's like the pre-thesis defense, where you lay out what your project's going to be, then argue why it's worthwhile and why it's going to work." She swallowed some more of the margarita, the tequila going down smoother. "There is a slim chance he'll shoot me down, but I researched the fuck out of this thing. The only thing he'd pick on is the presentation itself, but I have time to smooth out the rough edges on that. I just need to make sure not to let him get to me in the meantime."

"You could just wait until your regular adviser got better," Rachel said.

"There isn't a guarantee she'll get better," Ani said, sighing. "I hope she does, and I think she will. But I've spent this much time, and I'm ready. I want to make my PhD."

Not to mention prove to her parents that yes, she was intent — and ready — to actually earn her doctorate.

The third Frost sister, Cressida, drifted over to the couch, sitting on it and tucking her feet beneath her.

"Aversion therapy," she said with a smile. Ani noticed that Cressida never drank.

"What do you mean?"

"I've been trying aversion therapy to get outside," Cressida said. "It's just a matter of taking small steps. The guy is an asshat. You're having trouble with him. Just make it small increments, or small increments with some different asshat," Cressida said, her smile broadening. "And then you'll get used to it before you know it."

"Asshole aversion therapy," Ani snickered. Tessa burst into laughter.

"As it happens, I have a house full of quasi-sexist asshats that you can practice with," Tessa offered.

Ani rolled her eyes. "I've met your coworkers, thanks," she said, but in the meantime, she smiled at Cressida. "How's your aversion therapy going?"

Cressida shrugged, but her eyes were cautiously optimistic. "I made it to the front yard," she said. "Hung out there for about half an hour. I mean, I still had to retreat to my room, but I'm figuring out places where I feel safe."

"You're doing fine," Hailey said. "There's no rush." She and Rachel looked like they were trying to play it off casually, but their eyes were either misting or bright with pride.

This is why I love this place, and these people.

After several margaritas (and a promise to Tessa that she'd crash over in the spare bedroom at her place rather than drive home), she felt much, much better.

At around nine, their friend Kyla came through the door in a bustle of energy. "Oh, good! You're all here. I made the alterations that I wanted to, some samples for a theater production. I worked on it almost all last night. I just had to show them to somebody!"

"All night?" Ani repeated, frowning. "Where's Jericho?" Normally, Kyla didn't spend all-nighters doing costume stuff when her hot, hunky boyfriend was home.

"He's in Vegas," Kyla clarified. "He's helping his friend Mike move from there to here. Mike and his son are going to be taking over the other half of our building for more serious custom work. Jericho and Billy are expanding the auto shop because business has been going well, and with Mike in the mix, they're really going to kick ass. Also, I'll be able to really focus on the costume stuff full time." Her smile was like sunshine. "Still, I wish that he'd been home last night, because these costumes are *hella* sexy."

Ani watched as Kyla pulled stuff out of the bag.

Tessa and Cressida crowded on either side of her to see, while Rachel hovered over her shoulder. Kyla distributed them around.

Ani held up a costume and gasped. There was what looked like a bikini made of leaves from the almost metallic pleather, in deep russet red, emerald green, and tarnished bronze. The matching full-face mask looked like a late autumn sun fabricated from burnt gold. It looked like it belonged to an autumn war goddess.

"Holy crap," Tessa said.

The next was what looked like a black corset bodice over pleather pants with a long half overskirt. It made her... respond, she realized. The corresponding silver filigree half-mask was stunning.

She wanted it, Ani realized immediately. More to the point, she wanted to be the kind of woman who wore it.

"That is some of your best work, Kyla," Rachel said, while Cressida clapped her hands. "Seriously. This is next-level, auteur stuff."

"I love Jericho beyond anything," Kyla said earnestly. "Being honest — since I, well, started having sex with Jericho? My work has hit a whole new gear." Her smile was one of pure, cat-like satisfaction.

"Maybe that's what I need to get my proposal presentation to the next level," Ani said, then winced as she realized she'd said it out loud. "Not sex with Jericho! Just... you know. Sex."

"Been a while, huh?" Tessa commiserated.

"It doesn't rival your dry spell pre-Adam, but yeah, been at least a year," Ani admitted. "Beyond that, though... I mean, I haven't dressed up, haven't gone out dancing. Haven't picked up or been picked up by a guy for ages."

Kyla smiled. "I've got just the answer."

Ani did not like the sound of that. "What did you have in mind?"

"Erotic City Con."

Ani's eyes widened. This was not where she thought Kyla was going to go with her suggestion. "What the heck is Erotic City Con?"

"It's this festival that celebrates all kinds of sexy stuff, that has more of a storybook kind of aura. I think that goddesses and mythology are part of the theme this year, anyway. You could borrow one of the costumes — I won't need them for a while, and I'm pretty sure at least one is your size. You're built like a model."

Ani bit her lip, looking at the outfits.

Kyla looked concerned. "All I'm saying is, you might want to try dressing up and hanging out. You don't have to have sex — I don't think this is just some orgy or anything. But it might be nice to be someone else for a bit. And if you feel sexy, maybe even wind up getting a little something-something... well, why not?"

"Why not?" Ani murmured, staring at the dress — and the mask.

For one night, she could be someone else. Do something completely for herself. Blow off some steam before she dove headfirst into the crush of being a TA, an RA, and doing her own lab work after the presentation was done and approved.

She needed this, she agreed.

So why not?

What kind of trouble could she get into, after all, right?

CHAPTER 2

Abraham woke on a sofa bed in a state of vicious hangover. He'd slept in worse places, and he'd had worse hangovers, but this wouldn't be so bad if it weren't for the pounding.

It took him a second to realize the pounding wasn't coming from his head. There was someone in the kitchen making all that noise.

As close as he was to Adam and Tessa, he was more than ready to tear the head off whoever it was to make them stop. "What the actual fu..." he started to yell, then stopped abruptly.

It was Tessa's friend Ani. He'd met her a few times, briefly. Each time, she'd looked at him like he had some particularly virulent strain of leprosy, and since he was pretty sure that she worked with that kind of shit, she ought to know. Her long black hair was braided, sort of, but she'd obviously slept on it, so pieces stuck out haphazardly. She was wearing a T-shirt that said University of Washington Huskies on it, and her dark skin tone was a little green.

"Not so loud," she croaked, gripping one temple and then wincing as she hit herself with the handle of the mallet.

"Not so..." He growled, low in his throat. "What the hell are you doing banging stuff so fucking loud this early in the morning?"

"I'm making a hangover cure," she said, and hit the cutting board with one more loud thwack that had them both groaning. "There. Sorry. That's all I needed."

He sniffed. "Is... What is that? Ginger?"

She nodded, then looked at him. "Want some? You look pretty rough, too."

He could only imagine what he looked like. He stuck his hands in the pockets of his sweatshirt. Well, as long as he was up, maybe he should make his own hangover cure. "What do you do with it?"

Her eyes widened behind the lenses. "Um, consume it?"

"Smartass," he said, but it wasn't as harsh as he normally would say it. "What, do you chew it or something?"

"Making chai," she said, and pointed to a pot of milk on the stove.

"Never had that. Don't plan to, either." He scowled. "Chai's something that teenaged, yoga-pants-wearing girls drink when Pumpkin Spice Latte isn't available. Real men don't drink chai."

"Wow." Her drawl was derisive. "Generalize much?"

He wasn't sure if her irritation was hangover based or what. "I'm making breakfast. I'll try not to get in your way," he added.

"I didn't know you were hungover," she said in a quiet voice. "Or I wouldn't have... you know, woken you up."

"With the banging of a mallet," he tacked on.

"With the *really quick* banging of a mallet *at eleven in the morning*," she clarified, her voice tight. "What are you doing?"

"Making breakfast," he said. "Best hangover cure ever."

"Making breakfast is more manly than chai?"

"This is." He pulled out some supplies that he'd had the forethought to bring over breakfast materials: bacon, sausage, eggs, hash browns. Bread. Before Adam had hooked up with Tessa, the whole crew would play video games until well past dawn the next day, then crash out, wake up, and have breakfast.

He glanced at his bounty. Greasy hangover food. Just what he needed.

He heard a gagging noise. Ani stared at him, eyes wide. "You're going to eat that?" She waved a hand at his supplies.

"Well, not all of it," he said, then remembered her offer. He figured he could be generous. "You're welcome to some."

She stared at the ceiling, as if asking for help from above. "You have got to be kidding me. I'll be lucky if I keep the tea down."

"Hey, this is a traditional, tried-and-true hangover cure," he said. "Short of having another shot of moonshine, eating lots of greasy food is the manliest cure for hangover there is."

She carefully poured the hot milk over the spices, putting in some of the pulverized ginger and then squeezing in some honey. "You've got to be kidding me," she said. "*Manliest?* Could you be a little more cliché?"

He paused. He'd thought they were having fun, but... well, if she was going to pull her claws out, then he wasn't going to go easy. "Well, there is one more cure that's manlier than bacon, I admit."

She grabbed her tea. "I don't think I want to hear it."

But she still paused at the doorway.

He smirked, waiting as he pulled bacon out and put it on the heating griddle. She still stood there, rubbing the mug.

"So, what is it?" she finally asked.

He looked over his shoulder, grinning, with a heavy leer. "It's a good, solid fucking," he said. "Endorphins. Great pain relievers."

He waited to see the sneer, the look of sheer disgust. He wanted to see it — throw it in his face. Let her act like a stuck-up bitch, he thought defensively. She was the one pounding shit at — okay, it was eleven, she probably was in the right there — when a guy was hungover. And making fun of bacon. And calling him a cliché, and treating him like he was garbage. Let her...

But before the sneer, there was a second of pure, unadulterated lust. Not directed at him, necessarily. Just... in general.

Well, well, well. Little Miss All That wanted to get some. Wasn't *that* interesting?

He shut off the pan and washed his hands. "The bacon can wait," he said genially, feeling the smile cross his face slowly, "if you want to feel better."

She blinked, and the sneer went into full effect. "You're disgusting."

"Hey, I'm just trying to do my civic duty, princess."

If she gripped that stoneware mug any tighter, she was gonna shatter it, he thought, grinning.

"I'd rather finger-prick myself with leprosy," she said. "I'd rather get it on with someone *dead*."

"I can lie real still if that's your kink," he offered.

Her look was poisonous, and he suppressed a laugh.

"Gee. I was just trying to help out."

He grinned as she stormed off, and he heard her slam her bedroom door — then heard her moan in protest at the loud noise. He finally chuckled, even as his own head hurt.

That had been fun, he realized reluctantly. It'd probably be more fun if it had been with someone who didn't hate him. But that was okay. He didn't much like her, either.

Of course, the fact that they hated each other didn't necessary preclude getting horizontal.

He blinked at himself, momentarily sidetracked from the pounding pain in his head. *Where the fuck did that come from?*

Which brought him back to last night's conversation with the guys, what he could remember about it.

He needed a hookup, ASAP. And there was something about a bet...?

The phone in his pocket buzzed, and he frowned, pulling it out and looking at the message.

Good morning! Remember, you promised, the text said. And there was a picture of Jose, Fezza, and Dennis all propping him up as he held a signed IOU.

He'd lost. To add insult to injury, he'd lost at Overwatch, one of his favorite games. He'd gotten sloppy drunk, and now his punishment was to enter this hunger games tournament to see who could get nailed first.

He squinted, studying the details of the IOU.

In costume.

Apparently, he was dressing up and going to something called Erotic City Con. And they were going to choose what he was going to wear.

He groaned, even louder, as he continued slowly making the breakfast. He hated dressing up. He always felt like such a loser. His father would call it childish, or worse, girly. He'd gone to plenty of comic cons, but he'd kept his role-playing to a minimum. And when he'd dressed as Sailor Uranus in January because he'd lost a bet, he'd been able to say that — he'd lost a bet.

His father respected bets. A man kept his word. And technically, he'd lost a bet this time, too.

Turning the bacon, he quickly dialed up Jose. "Hey, Jose?"

"Yeah?" Jose sounded wary.

"Tell me where the hell this fucking con is," he said. "And what I'm supposed to dress up as. We talking mech? Soldiers?" He winced. "I've still got military gear..."

"As it happens, we pitched in and got you the perfect thing," Jose said, and Abraham felt a slow, cold shudder of fear.

What would they have come up with to troll him? Chicken suit? Speedo? Chicken speedo?

Oh, sweet Jesus.

This was going to be bad.

"I may have made a tactical error here," Ani said, wincing as they walked around the fifth annual Erotic City Con. She was feeling sexy, make no mistake. In the outfit Kyla had designed, it was impossible *not* to feel sexy as all hell.

Maybe that was the problem.

Not that she had a problem with the venue. She used to go to sex clubs with friends when she'd done internships in LA, and she'd hit a few clubs in Amsterdam during her gap year, the pause in her education that her parents had absolutely lost their minds over. In her various adventures, she'd seen people getting spanked, people getting pierced. She'd seen people having sex on stage. As far as she was concerned, whatever got your consensual jollies off, go to town.

But she'd also been to enough clubs to know that, if you weren't in the mood, it was hard to get in the mood. And if you *were* in the mood, but there wasn't the right opportunity, it was a recipe for frustration. Right now, her libido was revving, but there was no click with anyone, and that seemed to drive her irritation even further.

She scouted through the crowd, looking for potential hookups. There were the tourists: people who had bought tickets and shown up simply to gawk and mock. They were dressed "normally" and tended to snicker or whisper behind their hands or make snide comments in low voices that they knew would be heard. They also sneaked pictures on their phones, even though it stated specifically on entering that there should be no photography. Ani ignored these men outright, even as several of them smiled at her, trying to get her attention.

If you went to a place simply to make fun of people's passion, she thought, you didn't deserve to have sex with her. Or anyone, really.

Next, there were the preeners, the ones who took care of their bodies and knew it. They strutted like peacocks, almost mechanically, their eyes sweeping the crowd not so much to search as to ensure that people were watching them. *Ugh*. Not her cup of tea, either.

Finally, there were more that were passionate and truly into the lifestyle. Many of the guys tended to be less supermodel, even pudgy or scrawny in some cases, but what they lacked in physique they made up for in pure enthusiasm. Most of them already had partners, male or female.

That was what she wanted, she realized. Not to be part of the lifestyle — BDSM hadn't been her particular kink. But she wanted someone to want her as passionately as these couples seemed to want each other — if only for a night.

"Would you like to be in a scene?" a woman asked. "Have you done dominatrix work before? That outfit is stunning."

She was wearing Kyla's creation. The woman was brilliant. She wore a pair of black pants that zippered on the side with a black sheer overskirt that only covered the back. Her top was a corset of black leather cups and a web of black lace and straps over a deep crimson brocade. It tied up the back, and sleek stainless-steel chains connected over her breasts, joining with a black leather choker around her throat. She wore her hair up in a messy, curly bun with a small top hat and tulle veil that barely covered the ornate stainless filigree half-mask Kyla had created.

"Thanks, and sorry... I'd hate to do it wrong," Ani told the woman, who nodded graciously. "Perhaps I'll watch it."

The woman gestured to a cordoned-off area where the scene was occurring — a woman had a man tied to a gym bench and was using a light flogger. Ani let out a silent sigh as frustration ratcheted up.

Anyone could make any costume sexy, whether it should be or not — sexy pharmacist, sexy gym teacher, sexy cereal box. Hell, she could have simply dressed in a bikini or something and bought a mask, as it looked like several other people had. But while she wanted to have sex, damn it, she wanted... passion. She wanted to feel sexy enough that a man would work for it. She was tired of sophisticated and civil, or worse, *convenient*. She wanted a man who was crazy about her. She wanted him to crawl for her, ready to beg for her. Someone who would drag himself across a battlefield, simply for a kiss.

While I'm at it, I'd like an endless vat of ice cream that doesn't make you fat.

The problem was, she didn't have the time or the mental bandwidth for long term, and the odds of her finding passion like that, for one night, were between slim and none. Even if she did find someone, she didn't want the hassles of a relationship. Not when her doctorate was on the line. Which resulted in her current dilemma.

Here I am: all dressed up, and no one to blow.

"Are you all right?" Adam asked protectively. He looked adorable dressed as Jack Skellington, complete with bat bow tie.

She grinned. Tessa hadn't wanted Ani to go by herself, so she dragged Adam along to this thing just to be Ani's "wingpeople." It was, in a nutshell, adorable.

"I'm fine," Ani assured him, wanting to hug him because of his earnest expression. She'd only known him for a short time, comparatively speaking, but he was like the brother she hadn't known she wanted. He was protective without being a jerk about it, and he made her best friend outrageously happy.

Tessa wandered over with drinks in plastic cups. She was dressed as Sally, with yarn hair interspersed with leaves and a patchwork dress, her skin tinted blue. "You sure you're okay?" Tessa asked. "If you're not, we can walk you to your car."

"I'm fine," Ani said, watching as a couple tied up a third, and another tableau was set up. "I already got the room. I might as well enjoy it."

There were several attractive men wandering around. One, dressed as a voodoo-styled guy with Day-of-the-Dead makeup and a top hat, nodded and walked up to her.

"Beautiful one," he said. "Come with me. The show is about to begin."

Well, she liked that he called her beautiful. That was a good start. "What show?" she asked, playing coy and refusing to take his hand.

He smiled. With the skeletal makeup, it looked menacing. "A sexual feast," he said, "like you've never seen."

Tessa's eyes were round. "You mean, like, where naked people are the table?"

"The table, the utensils... in some cases, the food," he said. "If you go to the private dining room."

Ani paused, waiting for something, some chemistry, to kick in. He was cute, she thought. She could work with cute. Maybe she was just being too picky.

"We'll see," she said, and noted his look of disappointment — and irritation.

And there goes the spark.

"You'll be missing out on a truly delectable experience," he coaxed.

"Sorry," she said, and turned away from him dismissively.

"I've got to admit," Tessa whispered, "I *am* kinda curious."

Ani glanced over. Her best friend did seem bright-eyed, which made Adam equally excited.

The two of them were too frickin' cute, seriously.

The crowd of people was headed toward the ballroom, where the "moveable feast" was going to be held. In their eagerness, Tessa and Adam moved ahead of her, and they were separated by the crowd. She listlessly followed them, not eager for the show, but intent on supporting her friends.

Maybe I should just go to my room, get those electric candles out, and draw a bath.

She noticed out of the corner of her eye two men going against the crowd. One was a shorter, muscular man, dressed as Wolverine. The other man... not bad, she thought. Not bad at all.

Her heart started to speed a little, and she narrowed her eyes, studying him more intently.

He was wearing a mask like Maximus' in *Gladiator* — God, she'd had such a crush on Russell Crowe in that movie! — except it seemed to have Celtic scrollwork embossed in it. This guy wasn't wearing a shirt, and he was wearing leather pants and boots. He was cut and looked like a brawler.

Her body zinged a little. Nothing sophisticated about this guy. Hell, he seemed barely tamed. He also seemed bored, moving away from the ballroom and the feast.

He noticed her. She could swear it. But he didn't do anything. Didn't seem to smile, although his mouth was obscured by the edges of the mask and a trimmed reddish-brown beard. He didn't nod. He didn't do anything indicating interest.

She sighed. Because of course he didn't.

Until he got to her side. Then, as she walked by, she felt it. His hand, reaching out. Touching hers. Holding hers, for just a second, like a test. An unspoken invitation.

Just like that, it was like touching a Wartenberg wheel, only a hell of a lot more powerful. She felt her whole body jolt, and her eyes snapped to his.

He looked surprised, as she was sure she did. His eyes looked a clear frost gray and hungry, burning.

She froze in place, her fingers trapped lightly in his hand. She could tug free at any time, but she was trapped, by the electric want in his gaze and the sheer desire that slammed into her like a freight train.

She didn't break until she heard Tessa calling to her over the noise of the crowd. "C'mon!" Tessa said, oblivious to the moment that had just happened. "We'll miss it. I want to see this, I think!" Tessa moved to her side, tugging on her hand, intent on heading to the ballroom.

Ani looked forward, going with Tessa's yank, breaking contact with the man... but before she could stop herself, she looked over her shoulder.

He was standing still, staring at her, his arms at his sides. He looked like he would lunge after her. But he didn't. She watched him until she got swallowed by the crowd.

WHAT HAPPENS AT CON

· ♥ · ♥ · ♥ · ♥ · ♥ ·

Abraham felt like someone had punched him. It felt unreal, a high-voltage shock to the system.

This convention was a huge joke, as far as he was concerned. If people wanted to do bondage or S and M or whatever, he frankly couldn't give a shit. He'd been with chicks who wanted to play *Fifty Shades*, and he'd been with one woman who really was a part of "the scene" as she'd told him (in a very high and mighty tone, he remembered). She wanted him to be dominant, which wasn't exactly a stretch, but to him it essentially felt like micromanaging sex — not his idea of a good time.

Basically, this con was a big Halloween party with some people fucking. He hadn't seen anybody he was remotely interested in hooking up with. Jose and Fezza and Dennis were there yukking it up. Jose was dressed as Wolverine, Fezza was dressed as a chauffeur (*"I'm Black Mask!"* he had protested vehemently), and Dennis... well, Dennis had been a douche and worn a T-shirt that read "I'm a non-playable character," which made no sense in this venue.

To say the least, they didn't quite fit in.

Well, technically, he sort of fit in. The guys had brought him the whole *Gladiator* thing — complete with the leather kilt-skirt number — and he'd drawn the line. He wore the mask they'd bought, and he took off his shirt and smeared some blue paint on his chest and his face, so he could look kinda Celtic, going with the scrollwork on their nearly *Gladiator* mask. He also conceded to wear the leather pants that Kyla Summers had made for him for a costume contest.

He just wanted to go home and play Call of Duty for a while, drinking beer. Maybe he'd hit up Tinder during the week or something, although that thought made him sigh dejectedly.

Then he saw *her*. Safe to say, all thought of Tinder, leaving, or even basic English went right out the window.

He didn't know who or what she was supposed to be. She wasn't being obviously provocative, not like the woman with the skull pasties, for example. (Which was pretty damned funny.) She wasn't naked. She was impeccable. Her outfit was black lace over blood-red fabric, a sort of corset. She looked like a Daedric goddess or something out of Skyrim, something evil and powerful, something you'd sell your soul to.

He wondered how he could sign up.

Her skin gleamed like antique bronze, contrasting with the shining silver filigree of her mask, which looked both delicate and strong. It picked up the iron details on her corset buckles and the buckles of her thigh-high boots. She looked like a steampunk goddess, powerful and untouchable.

Which, of course, meant he had to touch her.

Play it cool, play it cool. He didn't want to show her how much she affected him. He assumed that she'd probably be swarmed by that already, and he wasn't the type to go begging for a woman. He stood his ground. But as he passed, he couldn't help but brush against her. It was a move he'd done before, a sort of test. Either there would be a spark of interest, maybe a conversation, or there'd simply be a brush of flesh, and quick as it happened, it'd be forgotten.

This was... different. This was like touching a live wire.

He watched her walk away. She wouldn't go far — not if he had anything to say about it.

"There's my target," Jose said, distracting him. He nodded at the bar. "There she is."

Abraham looked at the bar, expecting to see some towering Nordic beauty with big fake boobs or similar. Jose tended to be attracted to the porn-star end of the spectrum, even if he struck out often. But this wasn't. This was a short, tiny bit stocky girl dressed as Chun Li from Streetfighter, complete with the pink dress and hair poofs. She also wore a thick pair of glasses.

"That one?" Abraham asked. There wasn't any other woman there, but he was too surprised and had to clarify.

"Yeah." Furthering Abraham's shock, Jose sounded nervous. "I like that she dressed as an old-school video game."

"C'mon, man," Dennis said, rolling his eyes. "Even you can do better than that."

Abraham shot Dennis a look. Fezza shook his head.

"I think she looks nice," Fezza said, then smirked. "And I get the sense that Jose here actually likes her."

"So, get in there," Abraham said. *Because the sooner you get a piece of that, the sooner I can get back to my woman*, he mentally added.

Jose hesitated. Actually fucking *paused*. Which was odd, because Jose was generally fearless to the point of stupidity. Even if his batting average was around zero, the guy still swung.

Jose's Adam's apple bobbed. "I think I'm nervous."

"Not possible," Abraham said, hoping to lighten things up. "Because based on the girls you go after, I swear, you must have titanium balls. Small ones, but still, unbreakable."

Jose didn't even crack a smile. "That's not bravery. That's math. You ask enough women, you get a statistical probability that at least one of them will say yes. And from that pool, you wind up getting women who are interested in doing the deed. It's a simple equation."

Fezza's eyebrows raised, momentarily distracted. "You gamed it out?"

"It is *literally* a simple equation," Jose repeated.

"I want to see the math behind this," Fezza demanded.

"I want to go find the chick with the skull pasties," Dennis said, rolling his eyes. "Come on. Who's with me? Abraham?"

Jose ignored him. "And it's worked — the number game worked. There have been a few glitches. I went for maybe two months without a match, and then I wound up with a weekend where I had five dates in a forty-eight-hour period. That was nightmarish."

Abraham snapped his fingers in front of Jose's face, sensing the man was stalling. "What's different? What's the deal with this girl?"

"I dunno. I figured I'd come to this thing and ogle and hit on chicks, but she seems different."

Abraham thought back to the Steampunk Goddess. He knew exactly what Jose meant... probably because he was feeling the same cocktail of fear and adrenaline.

"You've got to go for it," Abraham said, more sternly than he meant to. Maybe because it wasn't just for Jose, it was for himself. "You want this girl?"

"Yeah." Jose muttered.

"Then man the fuck up and talk to her. Ask her out. Even if she says no, you've got to try, or you're gonna regret it. Okay?"

Jose stood up to his full height, looking like he was bracing himself for jumping out of an airplane. "Yeah. Right. Okay, I'm goin' in."

"I can't watch this," Fezza said, shaking his head and turning to Dennis. "Let's go find Skull Pasties."

"I hear there's a bondage room with real fucking, anyway," Dennis said. He turned to Abraham. "You in?"

Abraham shook his head. "I'll be wingman," he said. "Then I'm doing my own recon."

"Right on," Dennis said, with a smile tinged with a leer. Abraham sighed. Sometimes Abraham felt like Dennis was one of those privates in the army — all balls, no brains, even if he was a decent coder.

They left. Then Abraham watched as the normally deliberate and over-the-top suave Jose walked to the bar — and promptly tripped over his own feet.

"Fuck me," Abraham said, rolling his eyes. Now? Of all fucking times, *now* Jose got clumsy, rather than just awkwardly horndog?

But before Abraham could get there, the glasses-wearing Chun Li was at Jose's side. "Oh! Are you okay?" she asked.

"Embarrassed as hell, but okay," Jose admitted, his voice normal, not the deep, "how *you* doin'?" hit-on voice Abraham had heard him use in the past. "I was going to buy you a drink, but now I'm debating just going off and hiding somewhere."

"Um... I have a drink," she said.

He watched as his friend's face fell. "Oh. Well, okay."

Her cheeks went pink. "But... um... I think they sell ice cream bars at a little kiosk over there."

He brightened immediately. "I really like ice cream."

"I like ice cream better than alcohol, actually," she said, then glanced down at her dress — and her stomach. "As may be evident," she muttered.

"You look awesome," he said. "Street Fighter is one of my favorite video games."

"Mine too," she said, and fidgeted. "I guess I should admit — I'm kind of a video game addict. My friends dragged me here so I wouldn't keep playing Overwatch."

Jose's smile was wide. "I may love you."

She laughed.

Jose gave the signal to Abraham — he had this — as he and the girl went to a food vendor to get the aforementioned ice cream. He heard Jose telling her that he was a game designer, which was not ordinarily a pickup line, or at least it wasn't one he'd ever used. He agreed with his father on that front: saying you were a game programmer wasn't quite the equivalent of saying "I live in my parents' basement," but it wasn't really manly, no matter how technically challenging or lucrative it could be.

Fortunately, in this case, Chun Li quickly said, "Video games? I may love you back!"

Well, holy shit. It looked like the beginning of something. Good for Jose, Abraham thought.

He could focus now on what he really wanted. From this moment on, he was here for one thing and one thing only. He was going to find Steampunk Goddess. Want — no, *need* — coursed through him like a drug. He'd find her. He wanted to find her. And it wasn't romantic, nothing sweet like what he'd just witnessed. This was bone deep, no pun intended. This was lust, pure and hot as burning magnesium.

This was a woman he'd beg to be with, he realized. Beg, and keep begging.

He was going to find her. With that in mind, he plunged into the crowd and started searching, a hunter seeking prey. But almost immediately he stopped.

She'd gone in, following the Jack and Sally characters, checking out the feast. He could go in after her and try to comb the crowd, but odds were good he'd miss her in the throng.

Better to lie in wait, he thought. Because there was no way he was losing her tonight.

CHAPTER 3

Ani couldn't focus on the "feast," more interested in the exit than in the writhing bodies, the delicacies placed around them or on them, the people nibbling and devouring. Tessa and Adam were looking at each other speculatively, and she got the feeling they'd be having a great evening once they got home.

Now, it was just a matter of getting them there, because if she could find that gladiator/Viking guy, she'd be having a hell of an evening, herself.

"You two should head on out," she finally said when the act ended. "I think I've got this. There's a guy I have my eye on."

"Are you sure you're going to be all right?" Tessa asked her.

"Yeah, maybe I should meet this guy or something," Adam said. "You know. Vet him."

Ani forced herself not to roll her eyes. "Because that would go over well," she said. "Having my one-night stand essentially meet my parents."

Tessa bit at her lower lip.

Ani smiled. "Don't worry. It's a hotel. Even though it's noisy down here, it's a lot quieter on the upper floors. I checked. You two know where I am. If I don't call in" — she glanced at her watch —"three hours to let you know I'm okay, you can have the hotel come to check on me, all right?"

Tessa sighed. "Just be careful."

"I will be." She hugged them both, then sent them home. They were so wonderful, she couldn't help but love them like family.

But tonight wasn't the time for it. Tomorrow, she'd be back in the lab. By Monday, she'd be juggling all her various chores, TA-ing, probably cleaning frickin' test tubes and running cell samples and doing whatever else her new adviser thought was applicable for his rigorous research team. She wanted this, this one night, just for her.

She scanned the crowd, looking for that shirtless gladiator Viking guy, the one with the copper hair. Just the featherlight brush of his rough fingertips had made her tingle, and the way he held her hand, like she was fragile… not a tentative, fearful touch, but still one with plenty of space, like someone trying to tame a bird or something.

Jesus, just write a sonnet to the guy.

But her heart kept pounding away, and she kept scanning the crowd.

After nearly fifteen fruitless minutes, Ani let out a sigh. She saw a number of men ogling her, or at least giving her a once-over. They weren't *her* man, though. She brushed past them, ignoring the pickup lines, the posturing.

Where the hell is he?

She went back out into the lobby, which was blessedly quiet and relatively cool since it was largely empty. There were a few people at the pay bar they'd set up, but most would probably be across the street at a real bar, where the prices were better. There were food kiosks shutting down.

Had he gone home? Simply up and *left*?

She felt a pang. Damn it. That would be romantically tragic and all — maybe someday she'd tell her daughter about "the one who got away," although in retrospect she probably wouldn't divulge "so I was at an erotic convention looking to get laid when this gladiator guy brushed my fingertips." What the hell kind of story was that?

But her body rebelled. Hell, her heart rebelled. She wanted to ball up her hands into fists and just start wailing at the unfairness of it all.

That's when she felt him. Not directly. He didn't touch her. But she could feel the heat of him behind her.

When she turned, he was there. He still wore his mask, just like she wore hers. He looked like he'd been deliberately streaked with blue war paint under the stylized Celt mask, some streaks in artistic grams on his chest.

"You," she breathed.

"Looking for me?" he asked, and before she could figure out how to answer it in a way that didn't make her seem desperate, he kept going. "Because I was looking for you."

"Out here?" she said, feeling like an idiot. Good God, that *chest*. She wanted to bite it. This was not like her. Her eyes started to move lower, and she schooled herself *not* to check out the package in the Viking leather pants. No matter how badly she wanted to.

Instead, she stared at those gray eyes. Like glaciers, or diamonds. *Oh, God, this man!*

"The ballroom doesn't have another exit, except for fire and emergency exits," he said. "I didn't want to take the risk of going inside, only to miss you and have you leave. I knew it would be better if I waited for you to come out."

"You set a trap for me." Her voice was husky. She barely recognized it.

"I wanted to catch you." He took a step closer. She could smell him. Some kind of cologne, woodsy. And maybe something like the sea.

Jesus, he probably smelled like Norway and testosterone and she was there for it.

You are insane, she chastised herself.

"Now that you have me, what will you do with me?" She knew she was teasing, but part of her really, really wanted to know.

"How much of you can I have?"

"I haven't decided." Was that really her? She'd liked sex, but this... She felt like some kind of diva. She felt like a frickin' queen.

She felt like *Beyoncé*.

"How can I convince you?"

She smiled, and out of nerves and thirst, she licked her lips. Nothing broad and obvious, just a quick flick on the inside rim because she was so suddenly parched.

She watched as his muscles tightened, and the thirst increased. He took her hand. "Come with me."

Oh, baby, I'd love to.

Her brain was quickly leaving the station and her body was taking over in a bloodless coup. Feeling like raw nerves and sexual awareness, she let him lead her to a corner. There were the remnants of a few scenes, and a few people were talking in scattered knots here and there. It was empty, except for a photo booth with a curtain.

"A photo booth?" she said. "More whimsical than I would've..."

He shut the curtain, plunging them into darkness. The booth was unplugged, she realized.

Their masks clinked, and she heard and felt rather than saw his frustration. She felt her mask get pulled up out of the way, then she heard his mask scrape against his hair. She felt his face with her fingertips. He had a neatly trimmed beard and chiseled cheekbones. Long eyelashes tickled her, and she felt strong eyebrows under her fingertips. She felt his mask pushed up on his forehead.

He pulled her across his lap, and she felt the length of hardness beneath her, between the layers of leather and lace. He was... sizeable didn't even cover it.

She knew it was impulsive, probably insane, possibly even dangerous. But she didn't care.

Feeling her way, kissing her way, she pressed her lips against his, pressed her body against his chest, and her thighs clenched him. She captured his groan in her mouth and her tongue flicked forward before twining with his in a full-body, full-contact, soul-devouring kiss that left her shaking.

"Holy shit," he said. "You... God, woman. You are amazing."

She didn't say anything. Because she couldn't say anything.

"Let me have you," he said.

"Here?"

"Anywhere," he said, and she knew he meant it. "I'll take you anywhere you'll let me."

She got the feeling that he'd have sex with her in the main ballroom if she asked for it. This man was pure sex and temptation and her body was throwing more than caution to the wind.

She needed to get away, quickly. She needed to get it together.

She needed to get *them* together.

You are unreasonably smitten, she scolded herself. He was just a guy, not a god. If she let herself get attached to him, she'd be distracted. She could have him, but she had to make sure that boundaries were maintained. She got the feeling he was the sort of man she could get addicted to.

She couldn't afford addiction. She could only afford one night.

"Upstairs," she said.

He nuzzled her neck. "What?"

She took a deep breath. "Upstairs," she repeated, pulling her mask down and tugging his down, as well. "I have a room. And I want to use it with you."

· ♥ · ♥ · ♥ · ♥ · ♥ ·

Abraham held her as close as possible as they made their way out of the ballroom, through the lobby, past the concierge and the wait staff and guests in various states of drunkenness. His intent had to be clear, based on the leers, smiles, snickers, occasional sneers of judgment.

He gave absolutely zero fucks.

Not that he'd ordinarily give a fuck, he tried to tell himself, but he'd usually be a bit more combative about it. Even he could acknowledge that. If somebody wanted to judge him, he usually gave them something bigger to judge him for. If they thought he was uncultured, he'd break out his redneck and go to town. If they thought he was stupid, he'd act like a brute. And if they then thought he was a thug, he'd usually kick some ass and "put the fear of Abe into 'em," as his father would say.

But tonight, there was literally nothing that could drag his attention away from the beautiful woman who had just fuckin' fallen apart in his arms. Who was clinging to him like he was her lifeline. He could be insulted, mocked, threatened, and he'd turn his back on it.

Because damn, *this woman!*

It was cliché, it was stupid, and he'd roundly make fun of anybody he'd ever known who would say this, but he had to admit — he had never, ever felt like this before.

He wouldn't call it love. He'd been in love before, or at least he'd thought himself in love. That was two years of torture, and he'd put up with a lot of shit (and given it in equal measure). If that was hell, this was heaven.

Therefore, it couldn't be real. Or if it was real, it couldn't last.

But right now, he felt like she could shoot him dead afterward, and he'd stand where she told him to while she aimed.

Stupid, his mind counselled him. *You're being fucking stupid*.

But in this moment, he didn't care.

When the elevator doors closed on them, they were alone in the car. He body-pressed her against the flat wall, kissing her hungrily. He reached for her mask, but her hand flew up, covering his.

"No!" She gripped his wrist. "No," she repeated.

He felt a little tug of... something. "Why not?"

The light was strong, and he could make her out in it clearly. She had dark eyes, a deep, velvety brown. Her black hair gleamed with rich amber accents, subtle but there. Her body — perfection, making the deep scarlet of that body-rocking corset of hers practically glow. And those thigh-high boots... he couldn't wait to take them off her.

But most of all, he wanted to take the mask off.

"The mask stays on," she said. "Yours and mine."

"But why?"

Again, with any other woman, he'd probably take it personally. He wanted to feel offended now. Was she judging him? Was she afraid he was ugly? Doubtful — he could tell that what she'd seen, she was into.

Was she just slumming? Was that what she liked? After all, he looked the type — dumb as a stump, a slab of man-meat to hump and dump. That could be it.

But it didn't feel like that. It felt like something else. How the hell was he tuning in to how she was feeling, when he barely thought about how *he* felt most of the time?

"What's scaring you?" he said. He had thought about adding a throwaway endearment — babe, sweetheart, angel — but nothing fit. Nothing would probably fit but her name.

Which she was determined not to surrender.

Surrender.

Was that it?

"Are you afraid of me?"

"No. And yes," she admitted.

He backed off. "I would never hurt you," he said, the words rough as gravel. "Not ever. You have to know that, okay? Or we"—and this was torn from his throat even though his body screamed against it—"we don't need to do anything."

She framed his face and then dragged him to her, kissing him as hard as he'd kissed her. "I know," she said against his lips. "I know you wouldn't hurt me. But if we don't do anything, I think I'm gonna die."

His heart raced double time.

The elevator dinged. They almost missed their floor. He stuck his hand out, letting it close on his forearm before the doors pulled back. They wandered, entwined around each other, kissing and stroking as they searched for the right door. When they finally found the room, her hand shook so hard she couldn't get it to go green. When she finally dropped the card, he knew it wasn't because she found him ugly or was slumming.

There was something else. Something he'd find out.

He'd convince her. He wouldn't push her — he wouldn't do anything to hurt her. He'd said it, and he meant it. He wouldn't fool her. But he'd show her that she could trust him. He'd take care of her. He'd see exactly who he was dealing with.

And by God, he wouldn't let her go.

He picked up the card, opening the room and gently guiding her in. When the door shut, he turned his back on her so he could focus. He pulled it open again, hanging out the door tag — do not disturb. Because if he had any say, they'd be doing this until late morning. Maybe even into the next night.

With that, he locked and latched the door and looked at her.

He wasn't sure if she'd be afraid. But she wasn't. She was reaching to her boots, unzipping them, kicking them off.

"No," he heard himself say. "Don't. Don't rush. I want to unwrap you myself."

He saw her throat bob as she swallowed. "I still want you," she said. "I've never wanted anybody like this."

He smiled. Then he ushered her over to the bed. She sat on the edge, and he undid her boots, unzipping them, pulling them off... then placing a kiss on each inner thigh. He could smell the scent of her orgasm from the photo-booth, and it made him crazed. He backed off, because he knew he wanted to take his time — he'd meant that.

But damn, the closer he got to her, especially now that they were in private, in a locked room with a bed (and a shower and a comfortable, thick rug and several walls... *Damn, body, slow down!*), he didn't want to screw things up. He wanted to show her that she'd made the right choice. He wanted to...

Impress her?

No. Not like that. Not that he'd ever felt that way before, either.

This was very confusing for him.

He pulled back, taking a deep, calming breath and looking around the room itself. The hotel was nice enough — conference upgrade, nothing sensational but not cheap or sleazy, either. King-sized bed, just the one, with one of those thick white quilts and a ridiculous amount of white pillows that he fully intended to use in creative ways. The lamps were square and stainless steel... both were turned off. He started to reach for the lamp, to turn it on.

"No, wait," she said, popping up on bare feet. Something about that was adorable. She moved with grace, a sort of sashay that triggered something in him — a memory.

If you start thinking you knew this girl in a previous life or that she's your destiny or something, you're going to have to kick your own ass. Seriously, this was getting ridiculous.

She moved around the room, turning on little electric candles in glass holders that threw multicolor patches of light around, much like the jewel-toned tents downstairs. It made it seem like they were in a stained-glass window, or in an oil painting. It also made the whole thing seem more dream-like.

Also, it made it harder to make out details, he couldn't help but notice. There were squares of color across her body, obscuring it.

"I want to see you," he said.

"See with your hands, not with your eyes," she replied, her tone a little sassy as she took off the top hat and veil.

"I do like the sound of that," he admitted... and then grinned as she turned, presenting her corset ties to him and peering over her shoulder, looking like a fuckin' steampunk pinup wet dream.

"Jesus, if I'm dead, I don't even care," he breathed, and she laughed. Her laughter abruptly stopped when he undid the ties, loosening the corset and removing it, leaving only the flawless bronze skin of her back. He curved his hands in front, cupping her breasts, which fit perfectly in his hands. He squeezed gently, tugging and circling the nipples that popped in his hands like hard pebbles. He groaned, kissing her back, pressing his cock against her pert ass.

She shimmied, undoing the side zipper on her pants and letting them fall to the floor. She was just wearing a pair of high-cut panties, lacy, flirty, barely even there.

He was hard to the point of pain. She was naked except for the mask and those damned panties. She reached up, pulling a few pins out of her hair and shaking, letting those unruly curls tumble free and wild. If she'd looked like a goddess of sex before, with her hair loose, she looked like an avenging goddess now, unrelenting and fierce.

He wanted to…

Well, he just *wanted*.

"You're overdressed," she said, still bathed in that colored light. She stepped forward, reaching for the fly of his pants and undoing it. Then she got to her knees, undoing the laces of his boots. He nudged her back, toeing them off. She pushed him to the bed, just as he'd done to her, and she stripped the socks and leather pants off him, then his boxers. He was prone naked in front of her. *Except for his mask.*

She started to move over him, her smooth palms rubbing him from his calves to his thighs. He groaned, his cock bobbing. "You don't have to…"

"Shhhh." For such a gentle syllable, she was surprisingly emphatic. He groaned again, lying back… feeling her mouth start to move over him. He jolted up.

"Do I have to tie you?" she said with a gentle chuckle.

"I'm gonna go too fast if you do that," he said, wishing again that he could find some kind of endearment that fit, that worked. *Or her goddamn name*. "Come on up here."

"Hmmm?" She let him tug her up… and then her eyes widened behind the mask as he turned her around.

She seemed to figure out what was going on quickly enough, bringing her leg over his torso and placing that amazing ass in front of him, lace and all. He tasted her through the fabric, and she shivered and lowered herself to his cock.

She closed her thighs around his mask, and he felt her tongue laving his rod, rolling around the head. He moaned, feeling her tight bud harden against him. They didn't go too long like that, but it was enough to get them on the same page — to show them what they were working with.

He was the one to break first... to pull her away. "I want to be inside you," he said. His voice was so raspy he didn't even recognize himself. He sat up, and she came off his cock with a pop. He tugged her up, kissing her back, holding her hips, then spinning her to face him. Face-to-face.

Mask to mask.

"Let me see you," he groaned.

She shook her head. "Protection," she moaned instead. "Condoms. There by the lamp."

He reached over and saw that this time, *his* hands were shaking. She seemed to notice, taking the foil packet from him and pulling out the latex disk. He leaned back on his elbows as she rolled it on all the way to his base and pulled the tip.

"Your mask," he said again.

He just saw her smile... then impale herself on him.

He let out a war cry of pleasure, echoed by her sharp gasp of need. She did a full-body roll on him, flexing her internal muscles. He pulled her against him, her breasts trapped against his chest. He kissed her hard, tugging her thighs flush against him, thrusting up hard with his hips. She wrapped her legs around his waist, riding each crest.

They plunged together, moaning and writhing. He gritted his teeth against the waves of pleasure buffeting him. He waited until he heard her let out a rippling, sharp cry and felt her inner muscles squeeze him like a fist. With an incoherent shout, he came inside her, shuddering before finally resting his head against her shoulder.

When he pulled back, he realized his mask might be poking her, so he lifted it. She wanted her anonymity, fine. But that didn't mean he had to. She would need to learn to deal with him, he thought. Especially after what they'd just done.

She was sighing, her eyes closed. Her mask was catawampus on her face, and he gently tugged it away.

And then stared, aghast, as he slowly recognized her.

"Ani?" he said, unable to believe it.

Her eyes flew open. Then she screeched.

Ani stared at Abraham in abject horror. "No, no, no, no, no," she muttered, rubbing her hands over her face and scooting back on the bed. "Not you. How the hell could it be you?"

He blinked at her. "Are you trying to hurt my feelings, darlin'?"

She backed up until she wobbled, almost falling off. She cartwheeled her arms before righting herself and hopping off naked, crossing her arms in front of her breasts. "Did you set me up for this?"

"Believe me, princess, I didn't know it was you, either," he drawled, his eyes alight with irritation. "So don't think so highly of yourself."

Of course he didn't know. Of course her one stress-release hookup would be with the sexist asshole who had kept her friend off the coding team for years.

And of course he'd be one of the best lays she'd ever had in her life.

This is so unfair!

She knew she had a taste for bad boys and, let's face it, jerks. She'd had a boyfriend who cheated on her when she was in high school. She'd graduated to a hard-partying guy in college who had taken a good deal of her money and had made her feel guilty for denying him. She'd had hookups before, too, but they had been quick, and while occasionally fun, they'd never been this earth-shattering, world-changing, mind-blowing experience that she had to admit she felt with Abraham.

Why? WHY?

"We will speak of this to no one," she said quickly, scouting around for clothes. She'd tripped on the duffel bag she'd packed, almost sprawling out on the floor. Haste and nerves were making her clumsy. She dug into the bag, pulling out an oversized T-shirt and sweats, thankful that she wouldn't have to ask for his help in lacing herself back into the corset. "You understand? *Nobody!*"

"You ashamed of me?" he asked. "Of getting with me?"

"*Yes*," she shouted.

She was still running around trying to get herself together and flee when she caught a glimpse of his face and saw the stab of hurt on his expression before he schooled his face back to its usual sardonic cast.

"Sorry it was so disappointing," he said, and his words were clipped. "Normally when I get a girl off a few times, I get thanks. But I guess that's not your style."

"It's not that. You're fantastic in bed. I won't deny it," she said quickly, mostly because she knew she couldn't sell that lie. The guy was a god in the sack, without question, and he had to know it. "Probably the best I've ever had."

"So, you're ashamed of sex?"

"No," she said. "I got a hotel room, for God's sake. I invited you up." *I just didn't know it was you!*

"Then what's the problem?" he asked. "Because as far as I can tell, the night's young."

She felt her shoulders tense. "Because... " She gulped. *You're usually a sexist asshat and you hurt my friend.* "You say things like 'manly' when justifying your actions. Or you tell people to 'man up.' You are super, unbelievably..."

"Masculine?" His face now had a wry smile.

She huffed out a breath. "We don't get along," she replied tightly.

He looked back at the bed. His naked body was gorgeous, she had to admit, all cut and taut. His cock was starting to wake up again, as well, which caused a corresponding longing in her own lady parts. "We seemed to get along just fine a few minutes ago," he pointed out.

She swallowed hard, her mouth suddenly dry. "That's just sex."

His gaze was hot, and he took a step closer to her, tugging the clothes she was holding out of her hands and putting them on the nearby dresser. "I'm not going to lie, either — that was some fucking fantastic sex. And believe me, I've had plenty."

"And *this* is why you're an asshole," she muttered, reaching for her clothes again. He stood between her and the clothes.

"I don't understand it, but I'm not gonna question it," he said. "You wanted to hook up. You've got it. And you could get a lot more of it," he said. "Even if you don't want anything past tonight, like I said... the night's young. Hell, it's not even eleven yet."

She bit her lip.

Actually, the more that she thought about it, the more perfect their little arrangement was. She'd wanted anonymity because she didn't want to get further involved. With a guy like Abraham, she knew there was no way in hell she was going to be involved for more than one night, no matter how great the sex was. She had wanted one night, just one hookup, before she buried herself in prepping for her thesis proposal presentation, as well as whatever "rigorous" research assistant duties Dr. Peterson might have lined up for her. She wouldn't have another chance for sex for a while, and then when she was actually working on her thesis, it was going to mean a lot of time in the lab, as well. And she was going to do whatever it took to get her degree and start making a difference.

She would take the great night of sex, and then they'd go their separate ways. Which, let's face it, was probably what Abraham wanted as well. He struck her as the hit-it-and-quit-it type. And even if he wasn't, he was the manly chauvinist type, who saw her as the feminist nerdy type. He wouldn't want anything long term with her.

She took a deep breath and gritted her teeth. "All right. Couple of ground rules."

He smirked in triumph, making her want to strangle him. "Name 'em."

"I was serious before. We don't tell *anyone* about this. Especially Tessa." She sighed. "Tessa's going to be so disappointed in me."

He scowled. "Why? I thought Tessa was my friend!"

"She is, but she knows how you are about women." It had taken months for Tessa to forgive him for the way he'd treated her, during their "code off" when Tessa had proven herself as worthy a programmer as Abraham. Ani still hadn't quite forgiven him for it, which was why she still felt badly now.

"And how am I about..." Abraham shook his head, cutting himself off. "You know what? Never mind. We'll just get into a fight, and that's not what I'm here for. Any other conditions?"

"Yeah. After tonight, we're done."

"What? *Why*?"

"Because I'm not going to have the time," she said. "I've got a shit-ton of work to do to get my doctorate, and I'm going to be buried under a mountain of stress. I'm barely going to have time to bathe, much less bounce on some guy."

He grinned. "Huh. You study Ebola and shit, right?"

"Infectious diseases. Although right now I'm studying HIV and AIDS," she said, then huffed. "And it's not important, because we're not talking. We're not having a conversation. We're not going to get to know each other. This is strictly sex, got it? Tab A, slot B."

"Any other slots?" he said with a grin.

"Mouth, but otherwise, not tonight, bucko," she muttered. What was it with guys and anal, anyway?

"Duly noted. Okay, no personal chitchat," he said. "But Ani..."

She tilted her head, sighing. "Yeah?"

He moved closer, and she could feel the heat of him, hypnotizing her. He scooped her up like she was a feather, burying his face in her neck, nibbling at her collarbone. She took in a shuddering breath, feeling herself getting drawn under his spell, *again*.

"You said that we'd be done because you'd be too busy," he murmured against her skin, laying her down on the bed and then covering her with his body. "And you don't want to tell anybody because you think we don't get along. But do you really think that you'll be able to give all this up after one long night?"

She bit his lip, causing him to jerk, then laugh. "What happens at con stays at con," she muttered. "Now shut up and fuck me."

CHAPTER 4

"Fess up. Who got laid on Friday?" Dennis asked, rubbing his hands together.

Abraham glanced around for Tessa. She was off talking to a designer, not hanging out in the pit with the other guys. "The bet was just dressing up and going to the con, right? Not who would get laid first? I thought we nixed that."

Dennis booed, but Fezza nodded. "Yeah. That just felt too frat boy creepy to me."

"Wimp," Dennis said, looking at Abraham for approval. Abraham frowned, and Dennis backed down a bit. "Well, I hooked up. And *dayum,* that girl was a *freak*."

Before he could launch into a full play-by-play, Jose spoke up. "I didn't."

"Really?" Fezza said. "Chun Li didn't really go for it, huh?"

"Her name is *Kelly*," Jose said sharply, and Abraham immediately noticed a difference. "And I'm dating her."

Abraham stared at him. If he didn't know better, he'd say the guy was in love. Which made little to no sense. Jose dated women once or twice, and then either dumped them or got dumped. The disastrous combination of his horndog ways, unrealistic standards, and short attention span were legendary. Jose was a walking cautionary tale for online dating.

But now he looked... calmer, in a way. Which, considering Jose's usual hyperactivity, was saying something.

"We went out Friday after the convention, then we spent Saturday together," he said. "And I'm taking her out to dinner tomorrow night."

Dennis started chuckling. "Third date, huh?"

Jose sighed. "This isn't about getting laid. She's different."

"Why *wouldn't* it be about getting laid?" Dennis asked, sounding baffled.

"You haven't known her that long. How is she different?" Fezza added.

Tessa chose that moment to walk in. "Don't do that. Don't say a woman is different than other girls."

"Why not?" Abraham said, latching onto the topic change. Besides, he was curious. Ani was unlike any woman he'd ever met, and he couldn't put his finger on why.

"It puts her in a competition she never asked for," she said. "You guys ready to keep working on the engine?"

"It wasn't that kind of different," Jose said. "I was just saying I'm dating a girl."

Tessa smiled at him indulgently. "You're always dating a girl," she started, then blinked. "*Oh.* But this time it's different? Because *she's* different?"

Jose nodded, smiling proudly.

"Well, congrats!" She gave him a hug. His goofy smile broadened.

"Pussy-whipped already, am I right?" Dennis said in a low voice to Abraham, shaking his head.

Abraham sighed. He probably would think that Jose was acting whipped, if he weren't so damned antsy to see Ani again. If that got out — God, the guys would have a field day.

He could see why Ani thought they were so different. He'd been offended when she said she was ashamed that they were together, but now he could see how he was embarrassed about his own feelings.

"You never said if you hooked up, boss," Dennis said.

He glanced at Tessa, remembering Ani's demand. *Do not let Tessa know*. That was turning out to be good advice, too. Tessa would probably be pissed as hell, and protective. Not that it was her business, but women's best friends were nothing to mess with.

"What do you think?" he answered Dennis evasively.

"Good one," Dennis said with a dark chuckle. "What was she like? A real freak? Like, public-sex nasty? Because some of those chicks..."

"What is this, lunch break? Jesus. Get to work, Sullivan," Abraham said, pointing to Dennis's cubicle. Dennis was still snickering, then went back to his station.

What was she like?

He sighed. Since Saturday morning, when he'd awoken to find that Ani had already left, he'd been crawling out of his skin. He'd admit it — to himself, at least — that the night with Ani had been the best sex of his entire life. He'd heard before that you could get addicted to heroin after one hit. He'd never believed you could get addicted to women, or one woman... but damn if he could get her out of his mind for more than a minute. He hadn't even been this crazy over Becky, and that was when he'd been a sex-crazed, hormone-driven teenager.

He should've been working, and he was lucky they weren't under a crunch deadline, because he could barely keep his shit together.

He found himself wandering over to Tessa's cubicle. Tessa had been one of their audio coders, a menial job that didn't take any hardcore programming skills. Being frank, he hadn't thought she was capable of much more than that when she'd started working at MPG. She had been a hermit, and he'd never seen her in action until the previous December. She'd made friends with the Frost sisters in Snoqualmie and volunteered to build a game to help publicize their store. She'd reached out and asked the rest of his team for help, and then, in working with her, he'd discovered she was way more talented than she'd let on.

When he got to her cubicle, she was looking a little frazzled. He'd told her she could do the update for one of their properties using her new engine, and she was thrilled. It was a big step forward in her career. Even Fezza and Jose were taking point and helping her on development.

"How does it feel to be leading a crew and working on your own game?" he asked her, and was rewarded with a beaming smile.

"It's great. Crazy," she admitted. "And there's still a lot to do and we're not even in the deadline crunch yet."

"You'll make it," he said, without a trace of doubt in his voice. Then he grinned at her. "Or else I'll kick your ass."

She chuckled, as he'd hoped, shaking her head. She'd never been intimidated by him. She'd been way too shy and introverted, but she'd never been cowed. He liked that about her.

Ani's not intimidated by you, either, he thought. She had confidence. Hell — she was downright *regal*.

Was it any wonder she was ashamed of being associated with him?

He frowned, surprised by his thoughts, so he barely heard Tessa say, "I do need to leave early today, though."

He shook his head, clearing out his mental cobwebs. "What was that?"

She thought he was irritated, so she sighed. "I can come back later and make up the time. I was planning on staying late, so it isn't a big deal."

That surprised him. "How late were you planning on staying, anyway?"

"I don't know. There's so much to do, and I really just want to make more progress..." She had a stubborn tilt to her chin, he noticed.

He sighed. "Where do you have to go?"

The tilt inched up farther. "Does it matter?"

He felt his eyebrow go up at that one. "You're not sick, are you?"

"No!" she huffed. "Not that it's your business, but I'm taking some food to my friend, okay? Ani." Tessa blushed. "Um... you ran into her the other weekend, at our house. And I've talked about her a lot."

He felt his chest clench. "Is *she* sick?" *God, let her be all right...*

"Dude, nobody's sick," Tess said, rolling her eyes. "Well, except her original thesis adviser. Her new adviser is having her do an all-night experiment, where she has to check on something every hour or something. She's afraid of missing a check-in."

"Sounds important," he said, feeling stupid.

"Sounds like the guy is trying to set her up to fail to me," Tessa said, and Abraham felt a burst of anger blast through him. "Anyway, I was going to grab some takeout and run it over to the college, in Maple Valley. Shouldn't take me too long."

Taking food to Ani? Taking *care* of Ani?

He felt an idea hit him.

"If you leave now, you're gonna break your flow," he said, fighting to sound casual. "And there's a lot of time wasted when you gear back up after switching tasks. You don't want to be here too late, especially this early in a project. That's how burnout happens, and this is your first big project."

"You want me to just let my best friend starve?" Tessa began, but he held up a hand, stopping her.

"Just tell me what to grab and where to take it," he said, then watched her eyes widen. "What?" he finally asked after a few moments of startled staring.

Her eyes narrowed. "What's in it for you?"

He barked out a laugh, but it sounded forced to his own ears. "Cynical. Good. But in this case, I'm just trying to keep you on track."

She still looked skeptical. Time to break out some acting skills, he thought.

"I greenlit you, even though you've only been coding on the team for six months or so," he said dryly. "Keeping you focused is my job. And I'm not that busy right now."

That worked. He felt a little bad when she had a guilty expression, but the part of him that was still hungry for Ani didn't care.

I'm going to get to see her. He didn't know what that meant, but he was going to make the most of it.

"Just put in the order," he said, forcing down his impatience and eagerness, "and think of me as your delivery boy."

She laughed. "Okay. You win. I'll get you some money..."

"Don't insult me," he growled, and then saw her look of surprise. He fucked up, he realized. *Don't let Tessa know!* "I can afford some frickin' takeout, Tess."

She frowned, then crossed her arms. "Promise me you're not going to tease her or rile her up, okay?"

He blinked. Had *Ani* told her? "Why would I do that?"

"Don't act innocent," she said, and he felt well and truly busted... until her next words. "Adam and I heard you two the other morning, when you were both hungover. The two of you were sniping at each other. You and Ani get along like gas and fire."

Truer words were never spoken, he thought. God knows he wanted to burn with her again.

Now the trick was getting her to let him.

· ♥ · ♥ · ♥ · ♥ · ♥ ·

It wasn't even six o'clock in the evening, and Ani already felt exhaustion setting in. Dr. Peterson had come into the lab, his big presence — big ego, she thought with a scowl

— seeming to take up all the space in the windowless beige room.

"I need you to work on this experiment," he said, handing her a sheaf of paperwork. "And you're going to need to take notes — detailed notes — every hour."

She'd gone through the pages, then blinked. "This goes over twelve hours."

His eyebrow had gone up with disdain. "So?"

So here she was, taking notes on a frickin' petri dish of evil every hour, on the hour.

Of course, he didn't want her to be bored in that time, so he'd given her a number of other little projects to work on in the meantime. Menial stuff. She'd already washed the glassware and cleaned the autoclave, a particularly unpleasant little project. Now, she finally had a minute to herself, at least until the next experiment check-in. She had a timer set. She knew what she needed to do. She was going through her notes, getting her presentation ready.

Her stomach yowled, and she patted it like it was a dog. "Soon," she said. At this point, she was a bit nervous going to the bathroom in case Dr. Peterson came in and saw that she wasn't being diligent or rigorous or whatever other damned thing he wanted her to be.

Fortunately, Tessa was the best friend in the entire world. Tessa was bringing her malai kofta and palak paneer and a bunch of sides, which was the definition of delicious. It was a little thing to look forward to in what promised to be a sucktacular night.

The door opened, and she glanced up, hoping it was Tessa and not another one of her research team — or worse, Dr. Peterson.

But it was neither. She was shocked to see Abraham, his copper hair blazing, his gray eyes looking over her like he was starving and she was the first meal he'd seen in weeks.

"What are you doing here?"

He held up plastic bags. She'd been so shocked, and admittedly so focused on his face, that she had completely ignored the fact that he was carrying takeout containers. She sniffed. It was definitely the delicious scent of Indian food from her favorite restaurant, that was for sure.

"Tessa's hard at work on her game," he said, his tone a calm that belied the hunger in his expression. "I volunteered to play delivery boy and make sure you got fed."

She glared at him. "Surrrrrrre you did."

"I'd hate for you to be hungry," he said, and there it was, the hunger bleeding over into his words.

She took in a deep breath. It didn't help that he was wearing a T-shirt that stretched across a chest that women (and men) would probably write odes to. He looked like a posterchild for a men's exercise magazine. And the way he looked at her — like she was the only woman on earth, the only thing he'd ever wanted.

It was intoxicating.

It was dangerous.

She shook her head, both at him and at herself. "I made it clear," she said. "Just at con. Once we were done there, we were done. Period."

He studied her. "I just wanted to check: would you say that you don't want me?"

She started to say, "I don't want you" but she knew that her body would reject the lie.

"I don't want the complication," she said instead.

"That's not the same thing."

"You should have been a lawyer," she said.

He scowled. "Bloodsuckers. That's not a real profession — that's a blight on humanity."

She laughed. "But no, tell me how you really feel."

He handed her the food, and she put it on a cleared countertop. "Well, you've done your good deed for the day," she said. "You don't have to stay."

"I got myself some food, too," he said. "The tandoori."

She glanced at him. "I wouldn't take you for the type to eat Indian food."

His copper eyebrow went up. "Because I'm such a redneck?"

She shrugged, feeling embarrassed. Had that been the assumption? "You just seem like the type to eat raw meat with your bare hands," she shot back, and he laughed.

"I make a mean steak," he said. "Maybe I could make it for you sometime."

He was romancing her, or trying to. Trying to wangle for a date. She ought to shut him down, but the problem was, she didn't want to. Had he been the type of guy she absolutely didn't want, she'd have shut him down and then some. But there was just something compelling about this guy, and it was preventing her from being as harsh as she needed to be. He was giving her space, too. Most guys who were pursuing her would be too heavy-handed, coming at her from all sides.

Was he doing the same thing? Was she just cutting him slack because he'd given her six fantastic orgasms in twelve hours?

There was something to be said for a guy who could do that, she thought.

"You're thinking too hard," he said, and she scowled at him.

"I've got food to eat and work to do," she said. "You can leave at any time. Just take your food with you."

He nodded. Then he leaned forward. "I'll be honest: I can't stop thinking about you," he said. "And I wanted to see if you're still thinking of me."

Her mouth dropped open. "You've got a big opinion of yourself."

He shrugged. "If I'm wrong, tell me."

She rubbed her temple. "If I said yes, you're wrong, would you leave?"

"Depends. Would you be lying?"

"Is that something you'd decide?" she said, feeling anger bubble.

He shook his head. "No. If you say that you want me to go, I'll go. Even if you are lying," he said.

Suddenly, something popped into her head. "Does Tessa know? Dammit!"

"No," he said, his low voice irritated. "I didn't let Tessa know about us. Your shameful secret is safe."

She felt bad suddenly. If a man treated her this way, she'd feel like shit — right before she brained him with something and walked out the door forever. "You were an asshole," she said.

He blinked. "When, specifically?"

"When you wouldn't hire her. Tessa. When she was an audio whatever."

Now he looked shocked. "I didn't even know she was looking to get promoted. She was so introverted she was practically catatonic."

"She told me about the code-off and all that," she said. "You were dismissive. You hurt her feelings. She's my best friend, so I'm protective — and yeah, I hold a grudge." She swallowed hard. "That's why I'm ashamed. She's my girl. It feels like I'm dishonoring her by bouncing with you."

He tilted his head, his expression thoughtful. "I didn't think of that," he said. "Tessa doesn't still hold a grudge, does she?"

"No. She likes you now," Ani said.

"So, you're the only one who's still pissed." He grunted. "And Adam, kind of."

"I think she let you off the hook easy." Ani put the take out container on a nearby counter. "Tessa's more forgiving than I am."

He laughed, a rueful, short bark. "I like that you're protective," he said. "I am, too. And loyal, to friends." He glanced at her, looking her up and down, and she swore it was like her nerve endings started firing. His gaze was as effective as a physical touch.

He didn't move closer, but his eyes were hypnotic. "I'll give you all the space you need," he said, that growly rough voice of his brushing over her. "But unless you tell me, point-blank, that you don't want me to ever talk to you again, I'm going to keep holding out hope, darlin'. Because I have never been with anybody like you in my life."

She felt it like a jolt.

"So, what'll it be? Should I go now?"

She felt light-headed. She didn't realize she'd made a step forward until she was pressing him against a counter.

It was the pressure, she thought. It was the damned stress. That on top of a secret six orgasms from a man who made her head spin.

She kissed him.

It was purely experimental, she thought. The con had been special. She'd felt like a goddess — she'd dressed like one, she'd been in the persona of one. And he'd been a gladiator god. The two of them together had been supernatural.

Now, in her leggings and a dirty sweatshirt on her home turf in the lab, there was no way it could be as sexy, even if he did still look like a Viking god in a T-shirt and some jeans.

But as soon as her lips touched his, there was an explosion of sensation. It was *just* like that night, she thought.

No. It was even more so.

He gently wove his fingers through her hair, holding her ponytail in place as he moved her head, maneuvering it until he got the right angles for his roving mouth. His tongue swept forward, tasting her, teasing her, before shifting gears and devouring her.

She whimpered against his mouth. She didn't care who came in in that moment — her fellow assistants, Dr. Peterson, hell, even her parents. She wanted him.

"God, what is it about you?" he breathed against her mouth, his breathing ragged and gasping. He pressed hot, rough kisses against the column of her neck, spinning her until she was against the counter. Even though she was tall, at five ten, he still towered over her. She gripped his shoulders, first one leg and then the other wrapping around his waist.

His growl was lower and even more powerful. She felt the hard length of him pressing right where she needed him.

What happens in the lab stays in the lab, she thought. But no. What was she planning on doing?

"I can't have sex with you here," she said, her own voice breathless.

"Then where can we?"

She thought about it. This was stupid. This was really, really stupid.

"My apartment. After the experiment's over and I get some sleep," she said, wondering if it was mental exhaustion that was allowing her to make this rash decision.

"Where do you live, baby?" he asked.

She rattled off her address, then whimpered, grinding against him. "I wish I could do it now," she said.

He sighed roughly. "Me, too," he said. "But I think we might be able to take care of you a little."

Before she could ask how, he started rocking into her, the rough fly of his jeans and the hard length of his cock behind it rubbing her right where she needed it. She clenched her thighs around him, locking her heels behind his waist, pulling him tighter.

"Oh... right there," she murmured, her hips tilting her body, moving more quickly. She could feel it, her body clenching, building toward a climax.

"Come on, baby," he said, nuzzling the juncture of her neck and shoulder. He bit her, just rough enough.

She bit him back to hide her own shriek of pleasure. Her hips shifted hard. She heard the tinkle of broken glass.

When she came back to herself, she looked over. "What the hell was that?"

"I don't know," he said. "Don't really care, either."

She glanced over... then swore.

"The pipettes." She'd just cleaned a bunch of the glass pipettes... something Dr. Peterson had insisted on. "Shit! Shit, shit, shit!"

"Oooh," Abraham said. "Shit. I'll help you clean it up."

"Dr. Peterson is going to be pissed."

"It was an accident."

"He's not going to give a shit." She rubbed her face. This was because she'd lost focus, she knew. *Fuck*.

"You need to go. Now," she said.

"So that's it?" he said with an indulgent smile. "Hit it and quit it?"

"I don't know what it is about you that makes my brain drip out my ears, but I swear, I'm not going to fuck up my degree because I found a guy with a magic cock. You got it?"

He blinked. "What, you're serious?"

"*Out*!" she said, pointing at the door.

He grabbed his takeout box, then glared at her. "We're going to talk about this," he said, his voice tight.

"Just go," she responded. "I should've known better."

He left, and she cleaned up, feeling like shit. Dr. Peterson was going to be a beast about this. The aftershocks of her orgasm only made it worse, a reminder of what she was using to probably fuck up the most important thing in her life.

· ♥ · ♥ · ♥ · ♥ · ♥ ·

The following Friday night, Abraham was at his parents' house in Enumclaw, as he'd promised — or maybe *as he'd been coerced*. It was his nephew's birthday, and he didn't want to be that crappy uncle who just sent some cash in a card. He liked his nieces and nephews. He generally liked his family. His father had used his Marine pension and the pension that he'd gained after years of being a mechanic and engineer at Aircraft Dynamics, and now they lived on a small piece of farmland. His mother had a flock of a few geese, half a dozen chickens, and a demonic goat named Chester. Three of his five sisters were there, with their husbands. Two of his sisters were with his mother in the kitchen, cooking and otherwise chattering away. His father, his third sister, and all of the husbands were sitting in the living room, watching the local high school football team on Root Sports on TV.

"They need better defense," his father said, nodding at the screen. "Haven't had a good linebacker since you were at the high school, Abe, I swear to God."

Abraham nodded diffidently, drinking his soda. His father noticed, then frowned.

"There's beer in the fridge."

"Taking it easy," Abraham responded, then related his tale of the previous week's hangover, leaving out the part about propositioning Ani and the result of the "bet" while he'd played video games stupid-drunk. His father laughed uproariously, and the husbands nudged each other. Even his sister grinned.

His nephews came over to him, eyes bright. "Uncle Abe, you got any new games for us?" Carson, the younger of the two brothers, asked.

Abraham rubbed at his beard. "Maybe."

Terrence nudged Carson. "Told you."

Abraham couldn't hold out. "Look in my messenger bag. There should be a blue sleeve that has the demo for Cyberdinos."

"That sounds like baby stuff," Carson said. At eleven, he wanted to be as far from baby stuff as possible.

"Trust me, it kicks ass."

At thirteen, birthday boy Terence knew him well enough to trust him. The two boys sprinted off, each fighting to be first down the stairs.

"Video games," his father said, a scowl settling in on his face. "Jesus. That's a job? I was tooling aircraft parts when I was your age."

Abraham fell silent.

In the meantime, Jeannette wandered over to him, holding her hands high above her head. "Up," she said plaintively.

Abraham swung her up, enjoying her giggle, then rested her on his hip. He winced as she tugged at his beard. "You're prickly," she said, her tone and eyes serious. "Like our dog, Rusty."

He barked at her, then pretended to bite at her shoulders. She let out a scream of laughter. "Stop it, Uncle Abe!"

He stopped immediately, smiling at her. Over her shoulder, he saw his father open the first beer. "Let's go see what your grandma's cookin', huh?" he said, carrying her with him.

"There you are, Abe," his own mother said. She looked content, her smile gentle, her golden-brown hair tied back with a hairband so it wouldn't get in the way of her cooking. "I've got Salisbury steaks and mashed potatoes, and those green beans you like."

Jeannette still in his arms, he leaned over and kissed his mom's cheek. "You spoil me, Ma."

"God knows you don't make it home often enough, so why shouldn't I?" she said. "You got a girl yet?"

"And it starts," his sister Bette, mother of the boys, said with a laugh.

"I'm only thirty," he said. "I've got time."

His mother scoffed. "All men think that."

"Technically, he's right," his other sister Mona said as she took Jeannette from him. "Men can have kids much longer than women. Jeannette, honey, what did you get into? Did you find candy downstairs?" Immediately she whisked the kid away, already doing the licked-finger wipe-and-dab at Jeannette's face. It was funny to see his kid sister acting like such a mom.

"I'm not saying are you getting married. But you haven't even brought anybody by," his mother complained.

And this would be why he didn't visit that often, Abraham thought ruefully. But he held his tongue.

"Anyway, help put stuff on the table, will you?" she said, and he knew she'd be bringing it up again then. Still, he did as he was told. Bette called for the boys, who of course moaned and groaned before getting their butts up the stairs and setting the long farm table in the dining room. He helped his mother and sisters set the food out on hot pads, and the husbands took their places at various seats, discussing the prospects for the high school teams. His father sat at the head of the table, as he always had.

With a minimum of chaos, they passed around dishes, spooning vegetables or meat or gravy onto plates. "This smells delicious, Mom," Abraham said.

"Are you eating well enough?" His mother pushed a basket of oven-warmed rolls at him. "I'm always afraid you're eating nothing but cookies and mac'n'cheese when you're not here."

"You know I can't do without protein," he said, shaking his head and laughing. "I don't cook like you, but who does?"

"He's right," Bette's husband said, causing Bette to swat at him with one hand. "Hey! You agree with me."

"He's not wrong," Bette said.

"Besides, after the MREs I ate in Iraq, I figure mac'n'cheese would be a step up," Abraham admitted. "I eat okay. Probably eat out too often, but..."

"Why didn't you reenlist, anyway?" his father asked. "A military career would've provided for you long term."

The table went quiet. Only Jeannette started babbling. Mona broke up a dinner roll for her, buttering it.

"I told you, I'd spent enough time in the sand," Abraham said, keeping his voice steady. He loved his dad. They didn't always have this conversation, and he wasn't quite sure what triggered it tonight. He glanced at his mother, who looked both sorrowful and wary as she shrugged.

"Making games. A grown damned man." His father shook his head. "I just wonder what the hell you're thinking sometimes."

Abraham made a fist, but it was beneath the table. He took a few deep breaths, wondering if he should get up and grab a beer of his own now.

"Video games make more money than movies anymore, Dad," his sister Bette said. Bette was the peacemaker, taking after his mother. "It's a lucrative field. If either of the boys decide to go to college to become programmers, that's—"

"It's no real way to make a living," he yelled, and they all jolted. Jeannette started to cry.

"Jesus, Dad," Mona said, narrowing her eyes at him and picking Jeannette up. "Could you not?"

"You watch your tone, young lady," he said, but he was still glaring at Abraham.

"No, *you* watch *your* tone around *my* kid," Mona said, stepping closer to him. Mona was the baby, his little princess — and also the one who was most like him. She could get away with what the rest of them couldn't.

Her father stared at her for a second, then held out his hands. "Hand her over, would ya?"

Abraham froze. He could see Mona's husband, Ty, starting to get up, his eyes wide, his jaw clenched. Mona shook her head almost imperceptibly.

His father took Jeannette. "Now, now, hush. Grandpa just yells sometimes. You know, you yell sometimes, too. Woke me and your grandma up all the time. For a little thing, you sure can holler!" He hummed a little, then spooned a buttery bite of mashed potatoes, holding it out for her. "Want some?"

Jeannette eyed him warily, then nodded and took the spoon in her mouth.

It was like the room breathed a collective sigh of relief. The rest of the dinner went without incident, largely. Abraham helped clean up, and his mother brought out ice cream and a family recipe chocolate pie. Afterward, his father got into a heated political debate with Mona while Jeannette fell asleep. The boys were still downstairs, playing video games.

Abraham grabbed his messenger bag. "Gotta go," he said, distributing hugs all around. "Long drive."

"You could always crash here," his father said, even though his tone was still surly. "You know we've got an extra room."

"Messed up my back on Adam's sofa," Abraham said easily, avoiding his father's eyes. "But I'll probably be back before August, to help you with the woodshed before leaves start falling. Okay?"

After giving hugs and goodbyes all around, he went outside.

"Abraham, wait."

He turned, seeing his mother on the porch. "Ma, go back inside. The mosquitos are nuts tonight. You'll get eaten alive."

She shook her head. "He didn't mean it."

Abraham clenched his jaw. "He never does."

"He's just unhappy. He wants to make sure you're settled, you know?" She smiled weakly. "Maybe you can bring a girl by."

Hell, I want that, too! But the thought of bringing home a girl that his father wouldn't outright hate... How would that work?

"Yeah, well, maybe he can just..." Abraham stopped, let out another breath. "I'll see. Okay?"

"Okay," she said. "Love you."

"Love you, too," he said, hugging her. Then he got in his car.

He felt like a raw nerve all the way home. He knew he could let out some of his anger online, playing Call of Duty or something. But what did he do about... whatever emotion it was that made him feel like shit because his dad thought he had a pussy job and should've stayed in the army? When his mom's constant reminders just put salt in the wound of how lonely he was suddenly realizing he was?

He didn't know what to do. At least, not until a vision of Ani flashed in his mind, and he had an overwhelming desire to see her.

It wasn't just the sex, he thought. Not that he'd say no to sex — he wasn't stupid or insane or dead, and he'd probably need to be all three to turn down sex with Ani. But he just wanted to *be* with her. Even when she was prodding him, challenging him, he felt... well, he couldn't describe how he felt. It wasn't contentment, because they weren't at that stage. But he felt less alone.

Maybe that was all he could ask for.

He still remembered her address, he realized. Pulling over, he popped it into his phone's GPS. She might chase after him with a broom, or throw glassware at him, he realized. But the least he could do was try.

CHAPTER 5

It was nine thirty at night, and Ani was sluggishly eating some Thai food at her coffee table, watching reruns of.... something. *Law & Order*, she thought. She wasn't paying attention.

Her kitchen table was covered with all the papers she needed to grade. Golden Boy Jeffrey had dumped them on her after she'd had a blow-out with Dr. Peterson after what she was now calling PipetteGate. She'd known he wouldn't be happy, and he'd probably blow it out of proportion. Apparently, she'd underestimated his response, which she hadn't known was possible.

"You broke an entire box of pipettes! What were you thinking? How could you be so clumsy?" he'd railed, as if she'd somehow killed a small child in the process.

"It was an accident..."

"It's coming out of your stipend," he said. "The lab is not made of money, you know."

Yes, Dad. She bit her lip. She was well aware that, despite its great reputation, the lab was not well funded. Or so they always claimed when the researchers complained about things like the autoclave or the centrifuge breaking down in the middle of experiments.

"I'm very sorry," she'd said instead. "It won't happen again."

"You're damned right there," he had said darkly. "I'm going to need you to show me that you're not going to be clumsy again."

And what was his proof?

Today, she'd spent the better part of the day doing all the clearing, cleaning, muck work that only assistants who were being given the "Cinderella" treatment received. She had to clean out the pump oil and clear out the autoclave, *again*. She had to dump all the pee samples that were outdated. She had to clean the "poopshake blender," the blender that processed fecal samples.

By the time she got home, she felt sick to her stomach and she'd already showered twice and washed her hands raw.

Now, she was eating, and wishing she could sleep, but there were tons of papers to handle. Not to mention work that she needed to do on her thesis proposal defense.

A small — okay, not so small — part of her wondered if this was Dr. Peterson's way of hazing her. He hadn't said anything outrageously or actionably shitty, but he'd thrown lots of work her way. She knew that Linda was getting ground down, as well.

Is he really being a sexist asshat, or is he just being rigorous, one of those "tough guys" in academia that wants to prove how much his team can take? Is it all in my head?

There was a knock on her door, startling her. She walked over to her closet, grabbing her metal baseball bat as her heart raced. Then she peeked through the peephole.

Only one man could have that shock of copper hair, she thought.

And that beard.

And take up the peephole like Mount Rainier.

She opened the door, bat still in hand. "What are you doing here?" she demanded.

"Well, you gave me your address, but not your phone number," he said, "or else I would've called. Can I come in?"

She stepped aside before she realized what she was doing. Damn, she was loopy. "What do you want?" she asked again.

"You," he said.

"Well, you can't have me. You sure as hell can't have me tonight," she said. "I'm tired enough that my eyes are crossed and I can't see straight, and I have a bunch of papers I still need to grade."

"I didn't come here for sex." When she laughed out loud at that, he shrugged. "It wasn't the first priority for me."

She laughed again, harder.

"There were other issues I wanted to discuss as well, okay?" he said.

She shook her head. "I don't have the time or the inclination. I got in massive trouble just because of that stupid pipette box. Can you believe?"

"Seriously? Why?" He looked like someone had goosed him. "It was a box of fucking glassware. I'll reimburse for damages if it comes to that."

"My adviser thinks that women are too clumsy and hysterical to be in labs, apparently," she said, anger dripping from every syllable. "This only reinforced that. To prove I wasn't too clumsy, I've spent the day cleaning *all* the glassware and doing a bunch of other menial chores."

"What an asshole. Can't you—"

"Listen, I know what you're going to try to do, and believe it or not, I appreciate it," she said, cutting him off. "But I really don't need a man 'fixing' my problems right now. I don't need suggestions on how to deal with my asshole thesis adviser, or how I should tell him off, or how to tell the university about how I'm being treated. This is the job. This is getting your PhD. Everybody knows it."

He blinked at her. "Are you fucking serious? Why would anybody do this?"

She stared at him for a second. Honestly, since she'd been in the fifth grade, it had never occurred to her *not* to go for her PhD. Sure, she'd taken some time off for herself, but really, she'd always known that she'd be inexorably drawn back to science, to immunology or epidemiology.

Instead, she asked, "Have you ever watched *The Walking Dead*? Or *28 Days Later*?"

"Um, yeah. Sure."

"I was at a slumber party when I first saw *28 Days Later*," she said. "And you know what I thought? I thought, how could it spread that quickly? What were the scientists doing? Why didn't they have contingencies in place? I actually asked my parents, who were then pissed that I'd watched a zombie movie."

She smiled in response to his smile.

"This is like being a superhero, only in disguise. Superman can save a city, but he usually winds up destroying a lot in the process. So do all of them. This is rescuing thousands, maybe even millions — with no structural damage, unlike a regular superhero."

He let out a low whistle. Then he walked toward her.

She still held the bat, and she held it up. "Easy, buster. You keep your magic penis over there, got it? Or I'm going Ichiro on that bad boy."

He winced, taking a step back. "That sounds painful. Is it really that bad for me to be here?"

"What did I just tell you? I want this more than I've ever wanted anything in my life. You, sir, are a threat to that goal."

"That doesn't seem right," he said. "What, you're going to have no more sex for the rest of your life?"

"For the rest of my doctorate, probably," she muttered. Of course, that could take, what, two or three years? Maybe more? She sighed heavily, her body already aching under the strain and sadness of that thought. She did enjoy sex.

"What if I promise to leave right after?" He grinned. "I'll be quick. You won't feel a thing."

She hated that she snorted a laugh at that before locking her emotions down. She glanced around. There were dirty dishes in her sink, piled up because she hadn't taken the time to unload her dishwasher. The trash was overrun with takeout boxes because she hadn't taken the trash out, and she really needed to. She knew her bathroom was in a state, and her floor was littered with balls of paper from her thesis proposal mistakes that she'd wadded up. Her laundry bin was overflowing. She was wearing the same leggings she'd originally made out with him in, when they were in the lab. Hell, she was wearing the same T-shirt, and that had been dirty that day.

"Gah!" she said, wondering if she smelled. No, she'd showered, because it had woken her up, but... just *gah*.

"I'm not the type that can just hit it and kick a guy out," she said. "I need to feel sexy and in the mood. Right now, I feel about as sexy as a pool noodle."

"Pool noodles can be pretty sexy," he said, and she shook her head.

"No. I don't need a lover right now."

"So, what do you need?" His voice was growly again, and she felt her heart pick up a beat.

She glanced around again — at the piles of papers covering the kitchen table, at the trash and the dishes and everything. Then she sighed.

"What I need is a wife."

He blinked at her. "Um... don't think I can help you there. Even if I were the right sex — marriage seems a little extreme, don't you think?"

"Not like that," she said, finally putting the bat back in the closet. "I mean... you know how men who have big careers, like in the '50s, they'd have women who were taking care of everything for them on the home front? Like making them food and cleaning their houses and doing their laundry. That's what I need."

"You need that more than sex?"

"Sure," she said easily. "Because once I've had sex, all the problems are still there."

"But you'd feel a little better, right?"

She shrugged. "A vibrator could do the same thing, but it can't do my dishes."

He took a step closer to her, and she could smell his woodsy cologne. "You know a vibrator can't do the same thing I can, darlin'."

She gulped. He was right there — she'd never had this kind of response to her mechanical friend.

Then she had an idea.

"If you were willing act like my wife, help me out... maybe we could have that booty-call business, as well."

"That's awfully transactional," he said. "It's like you're getting paid for sex in household chores."

She nodded. "I'd prefer to think of it as open-minded," she said. "And at this point, the house is so awful that I'd be happy to have sex to—"

"No," he said, quick as a whip.

She stepped back. "I was kind of kidding."

"I'm not doing..." He stopped. "I'm not being a 'wife' just to get sex. As incredible as sex between us is. I want you to want me *for* me, not for fucking chores."

She frowned. "It wouldn't just be to have sex, but it would help me get in the right mindset..."

"I bet it would," he said. "Seeing me grovel? Seeing how far I'd go? Jeez. I thought you were different."

"Excuse me?" she said, poking him in the chest. "You came over to see me, pal. You wanted a little some-thing-something. Do you know how fucking *tired* I am, day after day? And do you know how hard it is to feel sexy when you're wearing dirty clothes and your bedroom is a mess and all you can see around you is chaos? Do you have any idea?"

"I don't have a problem with it," he said.

"Well, I do," she said. God, he was sucking her down another rabbit hole. "Listen, I don't have time for this. I told you what it would take for me to get in the mood sexually, and you're just pissy about it. So let's just leave it at that, okay?"

She walked over to the door, holding it open.

"Thanks for stopping by. Sorry I couldn't be more accommodating," she said, then tapped her lower lip. "Oh, wait! *No, I'm NOT.*"

He growled at her. "You drive me crazy," he said.

"Right back atcha," she said. "And the next time you decide you're up for a booty call — go find someone else, okay?"

He stepped out, mumbling, and she shut the door behind him.

Now she was stirred up, and she still had blizzards of papers left to grade. Damn that man, she thought, eating more noodles. Damn him and the horse he rode in on.

· ♥ · ♥ · ♥ · ♥ · ♥ ·

A week later, Ani couldn't remember the last time she'd felt so tired.

She'd spent most of the night doing the TA work that Golden Boy Jeffrey had pushed onto her, saying that Dr. Peterson insisted that she be the one to do them "to make up for the glassware debacle." As if one box of pipettes was going to break the bank. She'd replaced the pipettes, by the way, out of her own pocket. It had been her fault, he was right about that.

Or Abraham's, she thought, then winced.

She'd been trying hard not to think about him. He was pushy and Alpha and antiquated. And buff. Handsome, in a rough, press-you-up-against-a-wall kind of way.

"Stop it," she snapped at herself, rubbing at her eyes with her palms. She had one more experiment to do for Dr. Sadist Peterson, and then she'd be able to go home, put some work in on her own proposal, and finally get an early night's sleep. Maybe rest would be able to help her.

Of course, the few hours of precious sleep she'd managed to get in the past week hadn't really helped. She hadn't seen Abraham since he'd dropped by her apartment unannounced. After telling him off, she got the feeling that she'd never see him again, unless maybe she crossed paths with him at Tessa and Adam's.

But he was showing up plenty in her dreams. She couldn't get away from him there — in some cases literally, where he was chasing her through some moonlit forest and then when he caught her...

She shivered. Not in fear, but under the influence of something much more primal.

She'd had an orgasm in her sleep from the last dream of him. That was a welcome stress relief, albeit a weak echo of what she'd experienced with Abraham himself.

"You just need some rest," she chastised herself, then took the microfine ball mill out. This was an experiment for Dr. Peterson, one she wasn't familiar with and hadn't been given the details for. He just said he needed lactose monohydrate ground.

She wondered if he was just giving her busywork. She wouldn't put it past him, honestly.

She poured the material in the chute, then turned the dial to start the grinding process.

It didn't work.

She blinked. "What the fuck?"

She checked the plug — it was plugged in. She unplugged it and tried a small scale on the same outlet, just to see if that was the problem. It worked fine.

"No," she breathed, plugging the ball mill back in. She bent over, looking at the dials as if she were coaxing a wounded person back to life. "Come on, baby. Just grind a bit for me, please?"

"Well, if you insist," a deep voice intoned, and she yelped, leaping up.

Abraham leaned against the door, his hands in his pockets. "I came to grab you whatever food you wanted," he said.

She sighed. "I don't have time for this," she said. "I thought I told you to just get out."

"And I told you if you tell me that you don't want me, that you want me to steer clear of you because you have no interest in me whatsoever, I'll back completely off," he said, his voice sounding deceptively reasonable. "But you haven't told me that. You said that you were tired, and that if I'd do some chores for you, maybe we'd have a shot at it." He frowned. "It goes against the grain, but I'm thinking about it. Like I said, I'm into you. Hard."

She was so tired, and so frazzled, she said the first thing that came to mind. "I do want to make out with you, and more. But I don't want to have to buy more pipettes."

He chuckled softly, stroking her face and her jawline, his eyes bright. "Did they really make you buy those fucking things? Tell me how much. I'll pay for them."

"No, no, it's fine," she said, feeling bad. "It really was my fault, anyway..."

"You work too hard," he said. "If you've got time, let me take you out for a quick bite. You have to eat, right?"

She looked at the broken ball mill. Dr. Peterson was going to blame her, she thought. It was stupid, but he was going to blame her for not being able to "keep up with the work" like Jeffrey — even though Jeffrey had pushed off most of his grading onto her, even though she was being given shit work that undergrads could be doing. He was trying to force her out.

"Fuck. My. Life," she said, and to her dismay felt tears leaking down her cheeks.

"Whoa. Whoa," Abraham said, his body straightening and going the bad kind of tense. "You're crying."

"No shit," she said, knuckling the tears away. *Annnnd here's where he leaves*, she thought.

But instead, he took her into a bear hug, which was really the last thing she expected. "Do I have to kick somebody's ass?" he asked, sounding irate even as he calmly stroked her hair.

"That's so stereotypically male," she said, even as she giggled a little. Yes, giggled. It surprised her.

"Oh, really? What would your friend Tessa say if somebody hurt you?"

"Probably the same thing," she admitted. "But she'd work her way up to it."

"I'm a simple man," Abraham said. "Why don't you tell me what's wrong, then?"

"I'm exhausted," she said. "And I feel like I'm being set up to fail. My adviser wants me to grind this stuff, with this specific equipment — and it's broken."

"Then tell him it's broken. It's not like *you* broke it, right?"

"I didn't," she said. "I don't know who did. But he'll blame me, especially if I don't get the stuff ready for his experiment in the morning. I need this fixed. I need this done."

He frowned. "They should have more than one if this sort of thing happens frequently."

She laughed. "Sure. That would mean allocating more budget. Budget is always tight. And they'd rather just have some skewed data than shell out more — you wouldn't believe what research grad students have to go through to get their doctorates, I swear." She shook her head. "I will just have to see what he does."

But Abraham was looking at the ball mill, frowning. "If it's broken, what happens to it?"

"I have no idea. They could call in a repairman, I guess. Or send it out for repair, it's not that big. Which means nobody would get to use it. Otherwise, they'd have to purchase a new one, and I know they're not going to be up for that, but we need one, so..."

"How much could one cost? This fits on the desk. I mean, it's portable." He looked at it from all angles. "It can't be that expensive, can it?"

She sighed. "A box of pipettes, like the one we broke, costs sixty dollars," she said. "This is a four by five hundred milliliter gear drive two-liter planetary ball mill. It costs about five thousand dollars."

Abraham let out a low whistle.

"Yeah, that," she said, rolling her eyes. This was a lot worse than a box of broken pipettes.

He sighed. "I have an idea, but you'll probably hate it."
She blinked. "What?"
"I know a guy who might be able to fix this."
She felt her heart start beating faster. "Really? Are you kidding me?"

"No. He was a tool-and-die man at Aircraft Dynamics."

She let out a low whistle. Everybody knew AD. They were one of the biggest aircraft suppliers in the world. "What's a tool-and-die man?"

"Someone who... well, he was basically an engineer. But he could also build things with his hands, straight from the metal, with a lathe or whatever. Custom stuff. If you needed a part fabricated for a prototype, he was your guy."

"Was?"

"Retired."

She thought about it for all of a second. It would mean spending more time with Abraham *and* letting him into her life a little more... the door she'd closed creaking open even wider. And let's face it, he was going to keep disturbing her sleep.

But she wanted this fixed. And for whatever strange reason, she trusted him.

"Okay," she said. "Let's see this guy. I don't want to let this thing out of my sight or be seen without it. Dr. Peterson will kill me."

"It's a little far, but I'll get you back by tonight, okay?"

"Where are we going?"

"Enumclaw," he said. Then he sighed. "I should warn you — this guy..."

"What?" She'd seen Abraham at his hungover and grouchiest. How bad could this guy possibly be?

"He's my father."

She bit her lip.
Oh. Shit.

· ♥ · ♥ · ♥ · ♥ · ♥ ·

Ani told herself that the reason she was going with Abraham was because she couldn't trust him and because she didn't want to have to explain why the grinder had gone missing. At least if she went with it, she felt like she was still responsible for it.

What if Abraham's father breaks it?

Well, technically, it was *already* broken, she reasoned. It was broken before she got her hands on it, and she probably should have said something. But after the pipette stupidity, she just didn't want to. If she had a shot at fixing this, by God, she was going to go after it.

Which was why she was riding in Abraham's big-ass black truck, headed out to the wilds of Enumclaw. Big grassy areas were dotted with horses or cows behind their fenced… paddocks? Was that what they were called?

"Is it much farther?" she asked.

"Nah, it's just right up here," Abraham said. To her shock he sounded nervous.

"So, is it one of those big farms? Like, with cows?"

"No, nothing like that. My mom's got some geese, some ducks, chickens, and a demonic goat. Not a big deal."

She blinked. Geese, ducks, chickens, and a goat? "What makes a goat demonic?"

"Ever seen their pupils? They're like cats' eyes. Just unsettling." He shuddered dramatically, and she couldn't help herself, she laughed. "Also, he tried to take a bite right out of my ass once."

Can you blame him? It's a hell of an ass.

She kept her mouth shut on that one. God knows, she wouldn't mind taking a bite out of that ass. But now was not the time to think about that. She did *not* need a booty call when she was having an academic crisis.

Well... maybe she could use a booty call arrangement. *In general.* But she did *not* need one with a sexist asshat who was gorgeous as a ginger Norse god.

She frowned. Well... he hadn't been as sexist as she'd imagined he would be. He still had a lot of gender norms she found frustrating, and he was still persistent. But he also respected boundaries. And he seemed to be giving.

Of course, he could be gaslighting her. She sighed. It was confusing.

The plus side of having Abraham as a potential booty call was that she doubted she could develop feelings for the man. The cons: she would still be in a relationship, of sorts, with him.

Of course, it's not really a relationship. It's not like booty calls were, by their nature, public. It wasn't even friends with benefits — they weren't friends.

Then why is he taking you to his parents to get his Dad to help you?

Because he wanted in her pants, she reasoned. Also, fixing mechanical things was more "manly" than, say, washing dishes. But a little part of her wobbled.

"What are you thinking about so hard?"

She jumped, startled. Abraham was glancing at her curiously every now and then, otherwise keeping his eyes focused on the road.

"Nothing!" she yelped, then immediately realized she sounded guilty. "Nothing," she repeated in a more modulated tone. "I was just thinking — the closest I've ever been to a goat was on a plate, I think. I wasn't happy about it then, either."

He laughed. "I've thought about roasting Chester a bunch of times since that ass bite, believe me. Even threatened him with it. It's like he knows he's untouchable — my mom loves animals, so Chester's gonna die of old age." He paused. "Is your mom like that?"

"What, animal lover?" She frowned. "Not really. I mean, I think she likes animals as much as the next woman, but it's not like we had pets or anything."

"Why not?" he asked, sounding shocked. She imagined him, a young, red-haired boy, sleeping with some big dog.

"We were too busy for pets," she said. "Dad's an orthopedic surgeon, Mom's a trial lawyer. I was in a lot of after-school activities — piano, tae kwon do, and National Honor Society in high school. California Scholarship Federation, too."

"So, you never had a pet?"

"I think maybe a goldfish?" She bit her lip. "I won it in a fair or something, I think, when I was little. I also think it died — those are usually feeder fish, and they're not very healthy." Or so her straightforward parents had told her. She had been, what, seven?

"How about the rest of your family?" he asked. "Did you have a lot of cousins? Lot of aunts and uncles? I've got five sisters, no brothers, so it's like they're always swarming around with their kids."

She laughed. "Nope. No brothers or sisters. And... well, my family is mostly still in India, so we don't talk to them much."

Which was as blatant a lie as any she'd ever told. In a world of Skype and FaceTime and phone calls, for pity's sake, there was no reason that her family would be kept apart from each other... except for the fact that her father was Muslim, her mother was Hindu, and their respective families had never really gotten over that. Her family, such as it was, was more Western — a busy little nuclear family of three.

She tried to imagine what it was like to have a bigger, bustling family, like the other desi kids she knew who had aunts and uncles nearby, who went back to India for a month at a time on holiday, who had weddings and parties that seemed to be like Bollywood extravaganzas to a girl who mostly blended in with the white kids at her Irvine junior high and high school. Fortunately, now she didn't really have time to wonder, but it would've been nice to have the extra support, sometimes — emotional, if nothing else.

"Here we are," he said, then paused a beat. "Ah, shit."

"What?" Her heart clenched a little. "Is he not home?"

"Oh, he's home, all right," Abraham growled as he drove down the long gravel driveway. "But apparently at least four — no, *all five* — of my sisters are here. It's gonna be a family dinner."

CHAPTER 6

Abraham walked into the kitchen, where his sisters and his mother had converged. His mother's eyes were twinkling with mischief.

"Did you call all of them after I asked to see if Dad was going to be around tonight?" Abraham said, keeping the anger out of his tone, although irritation still bled through.

"Yes, I did." His mother didn't sound repentant in the slightest. Probably because she wasn't. "You never bring girls home. I figured we'd just get the 'meet the family' done early."

"Technically, I didn't bring a girl home today, either," he said, ignoring her responding eye roll. "I mean, yes, she's a girl, and, yes, I brought her over here, but that isn't 'bringing a girl home' with all the baggage and stuff."

His brothers-in-law were riding herd on the kids, playing with hoses and squirt guns out on the wide lawn, or watching the Mariners game in the house. His sisters had brought over mountains of food, from the looks of what was accumulated in the kitchen: potato salad, sandwiches, chips and salsa, corn on the cob. It looked like his father would probably burn a few burgers. He'd nudge Ani toward the sandwiches, he thought without remorse. His father burned everything.

His mother wouldn't be deterred. "You said that you wanted your father to help her. You haven't talked about a woman since Becky, and that was in high school."

"Yeah, and Becky wasn't a good example." He and Becky had been inseparable in high school. They had been Bonnie and Clyde, Sid and Nancy. In other words, they'd been massively unhealthy and codependent. He'd spent most of his high school years taking care of her, putting up with her tantrums, and dealing with her jealousy until they'd finally both gotten sick of each other, living together for the summer after they graduated. He'd signed up for the army. She'd gotten married. She was now on husband number two and child number three, from what his mother had told him — because of course she knew all the details. From the sounds of it, Becky was also still addicted to drama, possibly working on husband number three.

A little part of him still loved Becky, and girls like her — confused girls, ones that needed care, ones that wanted to drown in attention. But he wasn't eager to play white knight to that kind of emotional roller coaster anymore. And Ani, well, Ani hardly seemed the type who wanted to stir up trouble simply to see if he cared. If anything, she ran from trouble. And any emotion on his part, really. He frowned at the thought.

"What's this Ani like?" his sister Mona asked. "She's off with Dad in his workshop, so don't worry about her overhearing."

"She's pretty," his sister Darla said. "And so tall!"

"And really smart, right?" Mona added.

He frowned. What was he supposed to say? "She's... different."

"Different how?" Mona asked.

"She's really independent," he said. "And I guess she doesn't really need me for anything." At least, she didn't need him to "fix" things, she didn't need him for company, didn't need him for emotional support. While she might want him, she didn't seem to need him for sex, a fact that still rankled.

"That's got to be weird for you," Bette said. "She doesn't sound like Becky at all."

"That's not a bad thing," his sister Maggie added, burping his latest nephew. "Becky was high drama and high maintenance and high everything else, I swear."

"So why did you bring this girl here?" His big sister, Rebecca, tended to be more no-nonsense. She was often his favorite.

"Because she's working on her doctorate and her adviser's a dick who's letting her take the fall for some broken equipment. He's got it in for her." He gritted his teeth just thinking about it. "I knew Dad could fix it, and I figured he wouldn't mind if he wasn't going out playing darts with the guys tonight, or going out to the tavern to watch the ball game."

"You know your father doesn't mind at all," his mother said quickly, but her expression was shrewd. "How did you meet this girl?"

"She's the best friend of one of my coders."

"Oh — that girl, the one on the team?"

The one on the team. One. Just the one. That's how they remembered Tessa. *Because you've only got one on the team.*

Maybe Ani had a point. He frowned, then brought himself back to the conversation. "Um, yeah. Tessa."

"The one who made you dress up like a girl last year?" Mona giggled.

"I lost a bet," he reminded her. "But yeah, that one."

"How did you start seeing each other?" His mother pressed.

"We're *not seeing each other,* Mom." He shook his head. "We're just... friends."

"Right. And I'm the starting pitcher in the next Mariners game," his mother said with a wry grin. "Fine. Then how did you get in the position to volunteer to help her with this little fix-it project then?"

"I'd brought dinner by…" He winced as he realized his tactical mistake. His mother pounced.

"You brought a girl dinner?"

"Let's make this clear: this 'girl' is a doctorate student," he said. "She works these crazy hours — like me when I'm on deadline. She doesn't have a chance to go out and grab a bite to eat. Tessa — my coder — was going to bring dinner to her, but I volunteered so Tessa could work. That's it."

At least, that was it the first time. Sort of. And he sure as hell wasn't going to tell them how he and Ani had gotten together at Erotic City Con. He grimaced.

"Besides," he said, trying to nip this in the bud, "she already told me point-blank she's not interested in a relationship. She said she needs a wife, not a boyfriend."

That got them shut up… for all of a second.

"She's gay?" his mother asked, her voice lowered.

He thought about letting that stand, but he'd been ingrained for too long never to lie to his mother if he could help it — man, she'd trained her kids well. "She's not gay," he admitted. "She just doesn't want the hassle of a boyfriend. Said what she really needs is someone to support her. Somebody to help do the dishes and bring her food and listen when she needs it, that kind of thing. Then she said she basically needed a wife."

"She's not wrong," Rebecca said with a low laugh.

"Who wouldn't want a wife, right?" Bette said.

Mona shook her head. "I'll tell you one thing, if Craig did the dishes more, he'd be getting it a lot more, you know?"

"Mona!" his mother chastised.

"What? The kids are outside. Don't be such a prude, Mom," Mona said with a cheeky grin. "If guys did more housework, women would be less tired... and maybe more, you know, happy to see their husbands."

"Or boyfriends," Rebecca said pointedly to Abraham.

Abraham felt the gears in his mind turning. Maybe it was that simple. Maybe she was just exhausted.

He could help with that, he thought. He was a problem solver. And the thought of her, the way she was at Erotic City... He had to suppress a shiver.

All at once, he realized — he was in his mother's kitchen. Abashed, he looked up to see all of his sisters and his mother staring at him. Then they looked at each other, breaking out into broad smiles.

"Friend, my ass," Mona said, and cackled.

He felt a blush heat his cheeks, adding insult to injury. His mother hugged him.

"Why don't you have her come on in, and we'll have some dinner?" she said. "I want to find out more about this one."

Abraham tried not to let that sound as daunting as it did. But he was looking forward to this dinner like a root canal.

· ♥ · ♥ · ♥ · ♥ · ♥ ·

Ani looked around at the bucolic farm, under the gorgeous colors of a Pacific Northwest sunset, and wondered how something so beautiful could be hell.

Abraham's mother had taken her arm — literally linked arms with her — and introduced her to a wide variety of people. She'd had no idea Abraham's family was so large. It was a bit like going to a wedding... much smaller, obviously, but just as overwhelming in scope, especially with the flock of children running around. There was no way she was going to be able to remember all those names.

His sister Darla finally pulled her to one side. "Are you okay? Sorry. Mom was so excited to meet you, she didn't think about what it might be like to experience us all at one time."

"No, it's fine," Ani said quickly. "I just... there's no need for her to be excited. I'm not an item with Abraham. We're not dating or anything."

Now Darla's eyebrow went up in the universal sign of *oh, really?* "Trust me. The looks he's sending you are not just *I'm helping her with a science project* looks. They're more like *I'm looking forward to breaking in the bed* looks."

Ani felt her cheeks flame. Oh, God, was it that obvious? And she was hearing this from his *sister?*

There had to be a hole somewhere she could hide in, right?

"Oh! Sorry!" Darla's cheeks flushed, too. "Abe is constantly telling me I have no filter. I just meant that he doesn't look like that normally, about someone he doesn't have, you know, feelings for. And besides, there's no way he'd just volunteer to bring someone to meet Dad, either. He does stuff like that for the guys he works with, or the people he's loyal to... family, that kind of thing. I think the last person he did anything like that for was his girlfriend Becky, and that was years ago."

Ani blinked. "I don't know about her." But she found herself suddenly inexplicably interested. Tell-me-everything interested.

Darla looked to see if anyone was listening, then dropped her voice. Ani found herself leaning forward. "He was with her for over two years, I think. And she was..." She sighed. "Well, I suppose you could say she was batshit crazy, but it wasn't a mental illness thing. She just had this need to be rescued. Like, a pathological need to be rescued."

Ani frowned. "From what?"

"At first, from her home life. A bad relationship. Then, once she was with Abraham and things stabilized, it was like she just looked for situations to create drama so she could be rescued again." She sighed. "Got herself in all kinds of debt. Cheated on him with a drug addict. Bad stuff."

Ani goggled. Abraham, putting up with that kind of thing? She didn't blame him for being antisocial. Hell, if she'd dealt with that, she'd probably become a social hermit. "What finally got them to break up?"

"That's the nuts part. She finally married the drug dealer," Darla said, and Ani gasped. "She'd been practically living with Abe, and he came home and found that she'd taken all her stuff — and a bunch of his — and up and left. Got a postcard saying she was sorry. She'd gotten married in Vegas and they were moving to Costa Rica or some shit."

"No way," Ani breathed. This was Lifetime movie crazy. "At least she never went after him with a knife, I guess."

"She did. Couple of times." She shook her head. "But she was tiny, and she didn't really hurt him."

Ani quickly figured the woman did have some kind of mental illness, which was unfortunate. Still, Abraham had dealt with a lot.

"So anyway, we haven't seen him with anybody since that, so Mom just wants to make sure he's happy — and you're not, you know, like Becky."

"I can assure you, I'm not a victim of any sort," Ani said firmly.

"Dinner, everyone!" his mother sang out happily. "Come on, come on. I've already made up the kids' plates. Ani, you're our guest, so you go first."

Ani swallowed visibly. There was a lot of food set out, and the barbecue had obviously been going for some time. There were ribs, chicken, burgers, sausage.

"The sausage is homemade," Abraham's father said proudly. "Venison. Keith went hunting this past winter."

Ani felt her stomach turn a little. Everyone was staring at her like she was in a spotlight.

"I guess this is a bad time to tell you I'm a vegetarian."

They stared at her like she'd said she was a Martian. Well, except for his father, who looked at her like she was one of the infectious diseases she studied. Like maybe they should keep the children away from her, for fear of her condition being contagious.

"But the sides look lovely," she said quickly. "Is this potato salad? And the green salad..."

"Has bacon bits in it," Abraham's mother said, her face apologetic. "But the rolls are fresh, and there's fruit salad. And corn on the cob."

"Perfect." Ani quickly loaded up her plate with those items and took a place at the picnic table. Abraham sat next to her, his plate laden with all kinds of charred meat.

"Sorry," he muttered. "Jesus. Are you okay, being around all this meat?"

"Yeah, it's fine. It doesn't mean you can't eat meat. It just means I don't." She tucked in. "And these rolls are awesome."

Darla's husband, Keith, and Abraham's father and mother sat next to them, as the rest of the family spread out at the other tables. "So, you don't eat meat, huh?" his father said.

Ani nodded. She could feel Abraham tensing next to her.

"It's fine," Abraham said to his father.

"Oh, I know it's fine," his father said, rolling his eyes, then turning to Ani with what she felt sure he thought was a tolerant tone. "It's become popular. Lots of Americans are vegetarians, too."

She blinked. "I was born in Seattle," she said quietly, with a smile. "I am an American."

His father waved his hand. "You know what I mean."

Yeah, she thought. *I know what you meant.*

Abraham's father stared at her. "Vegetarian. Religious reasons? What religion are you?"

She sighed. "I'm a variety of things, actually. I don't like to label my spirituality."

He wrinkled his nose at this, obviously equating *spirituality* with *hippie*.

"What about your parents?" he pressed. Like he had a right to know.

Well, he had just miraculously fixed her batch grinder, so she didn't want to seem ungrateful. "My mother is Hindu. My father is Muslim."

"Muslim? In India?" His father's eyebrows jumped up to his hairline. "I thought India was all Hindus or whatever."

"India is very diverse," she said.

"Do you speak Indian?"

"Nobody speaks Indian," she corrected gently. "There are a variety of languages. My family is from Bengal and Jharkhand, so we speak Bengali as well as Hindi. Other places speak other languages, and there are tons of different dialects."

"Your English is great, though," he added, looking at Keith. "Don't you think?"

"Yeah," Keith agreed, before tearing at meat with his teeth. "This is great sausage, Carl."

She saw Carl's eyes lighting up for inquisition. Abraham's father wasn't going to be deterred, so she sighed, steeling herself.

"I hate it when you call someplace, like an eight hundred number or your insurance or something," Carl continued, "and you get somebody with a really thick accent. It's like, I can't even figure out what they're saying, you know? So annoying."

She gritted her teeth. "That must be."

"Honey," Abraham's mother said, from the side of her mouth. Her eyes were dark with warning.

His father leaned on one arm, poking at his food with a fork. Then he looked at Ani. "Your dad wear a turban, then?"

"Dad, Jesus," Abraham said, covering his face.

"What? Don't mind me, sweetie, I'm just joking." He frowned. "I am sort of curious, though. Does he?"

"I think you're thinking of Sikhs, not Muslims," Ani said with a sigh.

From the grimace on his face, she got the feeling he didn't really care about the difference.

"Right now, my parents are vacationing in France," she said, eager to change the subject. "They live in California. I try to Skype them when I can."

"Oh, I've always wanted to go to Paris," his mother said, her voice full of longing.

Happy at the topic switch, Ani smiled. "It's so beautiful..."

"Paris. Bunch of leftist cheese-eaters," Carl said with a scoff. Then he continued on his original trajectory. "You're a student? What are you studying?"

"Infectious diseases," she said, her voice short.

He looked at her askance. "Well. That's... well. Why would anyone study that?"

"To help people, Dad?" Abraham interrupted, his eyes flashing.

"I'm just saying, it's a double-edged sword, studying stuff that's maybe better off unstudied. Bad things can happen."

She looked at Carl, her exhaustion and irritation with his unchecked rudeness finally making the leash on her control slip. "Why don't you just come out and ask: am I a terrorist?"

Silence fell on the table. Abraham stared at her like she'd grown another head.

His father blustered. "Good grief, I..."

"I'm a grad student. I've just come back from a year at Helsinki. I'm going for my doctorate in Public Health. I'm studying to be an immunologist."

"What's that?" Keith asked.

"I study infectious diseases." She looked at his father. "Which means I have access to anthrax and Ebola. Handy, huh?"

His eyes widened.

She leaned forward with an exaggerated wink. "Just joking, *Carl*."

She sat, eating a forkful of potato salad, staring him down.

And then he started laughing. Not just chuckling. Like, roaring laughing.

"Holy shit," Abraham whispered.

"I like you, girl," his father said. "You give as good as you get. Bet you don't put up with Abe's bullshit, either."

"Historically, no," she said, feeling relief turn her bones to Jell-O.

"Well, you keep on doing that. I like a girl who's spunky."

Gah. She didn't like that, either, but she'd pushed enough tonight. She'd just count the moments until she could get the heck out of here, good potato salad or no.

Abraham put his arm around her back, squeezing her in a tiny little half hug, and suddenly she felt better.

"You watch yourself there, Abe," his father continued. "You're punching above your weight class with a girl like this. Girls like her don't stay with guys like you."

"Carl!" Abraham's mother snapped.

"What? I'm joking." But his eyes said otherwise.

Later that night, Abraham was finally able to tear them away from the bosom of his family and get the hell out of Enumclaw with a working ball mill. "I can't believe he got it to work!" Ani said, all but bouncing in her enthusiasm.

"I knew he'd be able to," Abraham countered, which was true — he had no doubt in his father's ability to fix things. What he had somehow forgotten was his father's — well, in their family, they called it "political incorrectness," with pride. When he'd met Fezza, he'd given him some shit about what country he was really from, since answering "Puyallup" hadn't done the trick. His father could be charming in his own way, but he didn't have a filter, and took a certain pride in not having one. He was an O.G. troll. He liked to push people's buttons and see if they'd take the bait.

He hated the fact that his father had made Ani uncomfortable. Knowing that he himself used to lack that same filter — and have that same pride — now made him feel like a shit. It was like he just hadn't seen it, or had thought it was some point of pride to be a dick.

What the fuck was I thinking?

Toughness, he thought. If you couldn't take some verbal abuse, then you were weak, and not to be respected. His father had taught him that, especially growing up in a house full of girls. He had to carry on his father's legacy, his father's stances. He'd gone to the military.

Hell, he had a good — no, great — job as a video game programmer, and his father still thought he was a pussy.

What the fuck *was* that?

"What are you thinking about?" Ani asked, startling him. "Because you're gripping that steering wheel like you want to strangle it, and I'd kinda like to get home in one piece tonight."

He shook his head. "No. Nothing." He took a deep breath. "Actually, it's not nothing. I'm sorry I put you in the position I did, meeting my family. And my dad's bullshit."

"He wouldn't be the first person I've met who thought they had the right to ask me about my background," she said, her voice mostly casual. Mostly, he noted. "I probably shouldn't have answered back with the terrorist thing, either. It'd been a long day."

"No, he liked that," Abraham said. "He likes it when people stand up to him."

"He likes it when people are rude to him?" she said, sounding startled. "Or was it the fact that I was a girl that I could get away with it?"

Abraham paused. He hadn't really thought about it, but... "I think if you're respectful, he's good with people standing up to him," Abraham admitted slowly. "But the fact that you're smokin' hot definitely did not hurt. He's got a weakness for beautiful women."

She laughed. "Sure. Beautiful in my jeans and a T-shirt."

"Angling for compliments?"

It must've come out sounding dickish again, because she sighed. "No. I'm pointing out that... You know what, never mind."

He felt it, that sharp sting. "You have to know you're beautiful," he said, his voice coming out sounding like sharp gravel. "You're the hottest woman I've ever laid hands on. Your eyes. Your smile. God, that body..."

He heard her swift intake of breath.

"I still want the hell out of you, but I'm trying to take it slow here. So, just believe me when I say you're hot, all right?" He knew he sounded disgruntled, but he couldn't seem to help it. "God, I am such an asshole."

There was quiet, and then he heard her let out a peal of startled laughter. "What am I going to do with you, Abraham?"

He turned into her science building's parking lot, next to her car. "I'll walk you up to your lab," he said as he shut off the truck.

"Why am I not surprised you're chivalrous," she murmured.

"I'm old-fashioned, and a lot of shit happens," he muttered. He started to get out of the truck, but she put a gentle hand on his forearm, stopping him.

"You're not an asshole," she said quietly. "Bossy, yes. Sexist, sometimes. Surly as hell? Definitely."

He snorted.

"But you listen," she said. "That means something. You've been nothing but helpful to me, even if you're sometimes kind of grumpy about it. You bring me food, you help me out, and you know what? You're kinder, and softer, than you let on."

"I'm not soft right now, sweetheart," he said, only because the thought of her calling him soft chafed at him. But the rest of it — she was grateful, he could tell. He could make out her features from the fluorescence of the parking light. Even in deep shadow, her eyes were large and doe-like, her cheekbones high, her lips full.

Beautiful, he thought. But also smart as hell, as his father had noticed.

You're punching above your weight class, boy. No way a woman like that sticks with a guy like you.

"Goddamnit," he said, then leaned over, getting close to her face. "I'm doing this because I want to have sex with you again. I don't know what it is about you, but I feel addicted. And if that means bringing you dinner or fixing your lab equipment or cleaning your damned apartment, then I'll do it. Because you are hotter than hell and I'm not finished with you yet, and I'll do whatever I have to, to prove that."

He leaned toward her, predatory, looming. Paused.

He was waiting, he realized.

Waiting to see how she'd respond. Not wanting to rush her. Wanting her to want *him* and be as much a part of this as he was.

Any other woman, he might've kissed to convince. But he knew thanks to her that it wasn't the right way.

And waiting made it that much sweeter when she leaned forward, twining her willowy arms around his neck and pulling him the rest of the way against her. He groaned against her lips, kissing her with all the intensity and pent-up longing he'd been bottling up for the past two weeks. His mouth pressed against hers, his tongue lashing out and parting her lips before delving inside, tangling with hers as she gasped and arched her back, letting out a small moan in response.

He cupped the nape of her neck, beneath her long braid, holding her taut against him. He wished he didn't have bucket seats, wanting to drag her across the gear shift and press her against him, straddling him. As it was, they were awkwardly but intently melded together, their mouths playing as his other hand roamed over her body and her hands clutched at his shirt, tugging him as close as she could. Finally, she put a hand on his chest, nudging him back as she breathed, deep gulping breaths.

"Oh, my God. You're so good at that," she said. "Seriously. You're like the Norse God of kissing or something."

He felt a little dizzy. "You are no slouch, either," he said. "Although you're going to need to give me a few minutes. I've got a boner here that I could joust with, and I don't think that's the kind of chivalry you had in mind."

She burst out into a chuckle. "You are insane," she said. "I really don't need you to—"

"I'm going with you," he said. "When is this fucking thing of yours done, anyway?"

"What? My proposal?" She sighed. "Another four weeks. I haven't had a lot of time to work on it, with all this other stuff going on — grading papers, and these extra research lab assignments..."

"Four weeks. Then you'll have a little more breathing room, right?"

He could see her eyes narrow. "Yeah..."

"Tell you what. I'm not going away, okay? But I'm not going to pressure you," he said, when he saw her jaw set and her gaze turned to a glare. "In fact, we don't even have to have sex. We *won't* have sex."

"And by sex, are we talking, like, legal definitions?" she said. "What's your angle?"

What *was* his angle? He just wanted to bag her, get her out of his system... didn't he?

He frowned. *Did* he?

"My angle," he said, "is to get to have headboard-banging, forget-your-name sex with you. But not when you're running at half power. I know what you're capable of, and I want it all."

She laughed. "Okay. I'll take that as a compliment."

"Four weeks," he said. "And I'll do whatever I can to make these four weeks easier for you — so when it's done, you'll decide to have sex with me. And we will fucking burn the joint down, for as long as you want after that."

She was silent, and he wondered if it was too insane.

"You liked it when it was a one-night stand," he pointed out, deciding to focus on the sex because... well, because anything else was confusing for him. "This is like a gun waiting period. Followed by a multiple-night stand. With benefits."

He'd never begged a woman to sleep with him before, and he felt a little emasculated. But he also felt a little shameless. She was worth it. More than worth it.

"I don't know," she said, picking up the grinder. "But... I'm more open to it."

"Oh, really?" he said, trying not to sound caustic and probably failing miserably.

She frowned. "You don't get to treat me nicely and then get sex. That's not how this works," she said. "I was exhausted when I was spouting that stuff off."

"So, you don't want a wife anymore?" he said, tongue in cheek.

"I mean, you don't treat me nicely just so you can have sex with me," she said, her tone serious. "You treat me nicely because I fucking *deserve* to be treated nicely."

"Well, of course," he said, stunned.

"And you get sex if I decide to have sex with you. They're not related. Too many men think that sex is transactional — I bought you dinner, you owe me, that kind of thing — and I don't want it to be that way between us."

"It's not." He nodded, eager to reassure her. "It won't be. I promise."

She got out of the car, and he walked around, taking the grinder from her. She glowered at him, but finally relinquished it. It was small, but it was sort of heavy and awkward. It wasn't a problem for him, and he found he liked carrying stuff for her. It made it feel like high school or something.

"I'm sorry I've been an asshole before," he said, surprising himself. "I mean, with Tessa. With you."

"Okay," she said, not contradicting him. He grimaced, then smiled. Had he really expected her to pretend that he hadn't been?"

"Hey. Maybe I can change," he teased. "You know. You could be a good influence."

"Oh, yeah, right," she said as they walked to the lab. "Because the love of a good woman is all it takes to turn a grumpy guy into a lovey-dovey super-boyfriend."

"Whoa. Who said anything about love?" he joked, wiggling his eyebrows. "Sex, baby. Sex will turn a guy into anything you want."

By now they were in a well-lit area, and he saw the look of sadness, and acceptance, on her face. "Yeah. I suppose you're right."

And he suddenly wanted very much to tell her that he was *not* right. He didn't know about love — when he'd been in love, it seemed like one big headache after another. But he knew that sex with Ani was phenomenal.

The thing was, he was starting to learn that *not* having sex with Ani was good, too.

He'd have to think about that.

CHAPTER 7

Abraham was still thinking about the night before — the kiss in the cab of his truck — as he ate his lunch in the break room at MPG. Most of the members of his programming crew were sitting on one of the big leather couches they'd purchased, parked in front of the big-screen TV, playing video games. This time, it was a demo version of Kill Zone: The Gauntlet. They were going head to head, on PVP mode. So far, it seemed like new kid, Dennis, was kicking everybody's asses.

"Anybody else want a shot at the champ?" Dennis crowed.

"Watch out, we got a badass over here," Fezza said, grabbing the controller from Jose.

"It doesn't surprise me that I beat Jose," Dennis said with a quicksilver grin. "I mean, you've been dating that chick for how long?"

Abraham noticed Jose's normally easygoing expression go tight with tension. "Two or three weeks."

"And you still haven't closed the deal yet?" Dennis shook his head as the game started up again and he spawned into the battleground. The split screen showed him on the right, Fezza on the left. "What the hell are you waiting for? She holding out for a ring or something?"

"Two fucking weeks, Dennis," Jose growled.

"Two *not*-fucking weeks," Dennis snickered.

"What about you?" Fezza said, obviously trying to change the subject as he frantically moved his character, trying to outflank Dennis's more powerful one. Abraham studied their strategies. He got the feeling Dennis was going to draw Fezza into a trap. "Did you nail that skull pasties chick from Erotic City Con?" Fezza continued.

"Nah. Found somebody even better," Dennis said easily. "Tits the size of grapefruit, I swear to God, and an ass you could bounce a quarter off."

Fezza let out a low whistle, and even Jose looked impressed.

"And you hit it?" Fezza asked, sounding skeptical.

"Hell yeah, I did," Dennis boasted... just before he blew Fezza away. "Booyah!"

"God damn it," Fezza said, relinquishing the controller. "Next time. Give me some practice, and..."

"Some of us are just naturally gifted," Dennis said, laughing. "How about you, Abraham? I could use a challenge."

Abraham finished off his lunch, throwing the trash away. He shrugged, then picked up the controller.

"So, you gonna see her again?" Jose asked Dennis, surprising Abraham.

"Who?" Dennis asked, as Abraham chose his character and picked his characteristics. "Oh, you mean Big Tits?"

"Nice," Abraham murmured, shaking his head. He had his moments, but if his sisters ever heard him refer to a girl as Big Tits, they would probably punt him in the nutsack. God knows what Ani would do in response.

Dennis seemed to take it as encouragement.

"Nah, I'm not going to see her again. We had a great time, but she got needy, you know? The next morning." Dennis shook his head. "I don't need that. Don't want it."

"Why not?" Jose asked.

Dennis was thrown enough to look away from the game. "Seriously? I'm twenty-five. I'm in the prime of my sexual life. There are a lot of women out there, and I am not ready to give all that up just for one. Besides... I have ADHD. It's like watching the same movie. I hate watching the same movie over again."

"Not even *Star Wars*?" Fezza sounded scandalized.

"How about you?" Dennis glanced over at Abraham. "Saw you wandering off with some chick in a mask..."

Abraham felt his muscles tighten, his whole body buzzing with tension — and anger.

"Did you hit that..."

"Watch it."

The bite in his words was like the crack of a whip. All the guys fell silent for a second, watching him warily.

He sighed. He didn't mean to show his hand. And what were they gonna think? If they knew that he was bringing food to this girl who barely gave him the time of day, they'd call him a pussy. *And they'd be absolutely right*, he thought with a grimace.

"If you're asking if I fucked her, yeah, I did."

Dennis let out a low whistle. "She looked hot as fuck," he said with admiration.

Abraham tamped down on the desire to ditch the game and just beat the shit out of Dennis IRL. "She was." *Is*, he thought. *Still is*.

"But you're not thinking of hitting... I mean," he quickly amended, "you're not going to go for a repeat there, right?"

"I am," Abraham heard himself say.

"Really? Why?" Dennis sounded genuinely shocked.

"Because she's fucking amazing, that's why."

Again, quiet. They never really talked about feelings, or relationships. The fact that they'd talked about this was the equivalent of a hair-braiding slumber party. Dennis seemed baffled.

"Did she do tricks? She was into the kink, huh?" Dennis continued.

Abraham sighed. He'd moved past anger. Dennis was young, as he'd once been — and hopefully dumber than he'd been, although he doubted it. "I'm not giving you damned details, man. What the hell is wrong with you?"

"I'm just curious," Dennis said plaintively. "I mean, I've been with women, and I enjoy them, but I have never been with a woman who makes me think, damn, I have to get me some more of that."

"Maybe because you're thinking of them as 'that,'" Jose said sourly.

"This coming from *you*, Jose?" Fezza said with a laugh of disbelief. "Mr. Tinder, King of the Horndogs?"

"I shut down my Tinder account," Jose said carefully.

"Pussy-whipped!" Dennis crowed.

"Right." Abraham had had enough. He dropped himself into game mode, his vision focusing on the screen, ignoring the prattling of the guys. He used Dennis's tactics against him, moving through the virtual jungle until he drew Dennis out. Then he slaughtered him in a rain of electronic bullets.

"Damn it!" Dennis said sharply.

"Never underestimate the big dog," Abraham said, putting down the controller. "Lunch break's over. Time to get some work done."

Fezza and Jose grumbled good naturedly. Dennis seemed a little pouty after losing the game. He glanced at Abraham. "Guess you've got some skills after all these years," he said. "Thinking of settling down, too?"

Abraham froze.

She's never gonna settle for a guy like you.

Then again, maybe that was exactly what she wanted. She said she didn't want a relationship, but she also said that the drive for getting her doctorate was making her loopy, not thinking straight.

Maybe she was waiting for him to man up, take the reins, and get them into a relationship.

It was decided. He was tired of being the nice guy. Nice guys got nowhere. He was going to go to see her — and then they were going to have some off-the-charts sex, settle on being some sort of couple, and he'd bet that they'd both feel a hell of a lot better.

· ♥ · ♥ · ♥ · ♥ · ♥ ·

Ani sat in Dr. Peterson's TA office, finishing up the rest of her grading. Or, she thought resentfully, finishing up the rest of Jeffrey's grading. Ever since Dr. Peterson told Jeffrey that she was going to be a TA also, he'd been shoving more and more work on her. Between grading and the menial shit work they'd been shoving on her at the lab, she felt like she could barely keep her head above water. It would be worth it, she thought. She just needed to get past this thesis proposal presentation, and then she'd at least feel a little less stressed. She'd still be struggling with shit work until Delilah was back in action — and she prayed that would be soon, for a number of reasons — but it wouldn't be as stressful. Her experiments could fail, her research could drag on for years, she could get sidetracked or set back any of a million ways, but if she could just get past her thesis defense, odds were good she'd make it and get her doctorate. At least, she had to hope so.

She had her fingers crossed for this one. She had her board together. She knew her stuff. It was just a matter of getting the presentation together, keeping it together, and proving it.

She was just about finished with grading a number of basic molecular cell biology 101 stuff when there was a knock on the door. Before she could answer, the door swung open, revealing a young man with sandy hair and a T-shirt, and a girl with glossy brown hair and a baby-doll dress.

"Are you Dr. Peterson's TA?"

"Um... sort of," she said. "I think you're probably looking for Jeffrey..."

"No," the girl said, her voice curt. "I got a bad grade, and when I asked the professor, Dr. Peterson, he said there was a new grader, and there was a good chance that there were mistakes. He said we were to come here to look at regrading."

"Yeah," the boy said, echoing the more forceful girl. "I mean, I think I could do better. And a bunch of us heard him — we can ask for a regrade."

Ani felt her heart sink. She was going to get out of here... damn it, it sounded like more people were coming.

"You all want these regraded?" she asked, feeling dread envelope her.

"Yes," the girl said. "When will we see the results?"

Ani bit her lip, grimacing. Then she frowned.

"How do you know I won't grade it harder?"

The boy looked shocked, then clutched his paper harder. The girl just looked pissed.

"That wouldn't be fair!"

"It's MCB. It's either right or it isn't," Ani said, rolling her eyes, and the boy relaxed. "If you really want me to, I'll go over them again, but I promise you, the answers won't change. Although — why don't you just have Jeffrey regrade them for you? He's your regular TA. That's his job, isn't it?"

The girl shrugged. "You're the grader," she said, then dropped her paper on Ani's small, clean desk. Within minutes, a small herd of students had tromped in, depositing their papers on the previously clear surface.

What the actual fuck, she thought, as her hopes for getting off early faded, getting work done on her presentation, and maybe — just maybe — cleaning up a little. She was hardly OCD by any means, but the state of her apartment was starting to get depressing, and she had enough to be depressed about as it was.

Jeffrey strolled in. "Lotta stuff there," he said.

"Please tell me you don't have more things to dump on me, Jeffrey," she said, allowing some bite to come through in her words. "I have a ton to do on my presentation."

Jeffrey stiffened. "You unhappy working with Dr. Peterson? Being his TA? Because I guess you don't *have* to be..."

She realized she'd have to watch her words very carefully. She could feel it — a trap, another fucking obstacle. "I just need time," she said, keeping her tone modulated. It wouldn't do to be branded the "hysterical woman" after all.

And didn't it suck that she had to consider that, on top of everything else?

Jeffrey shrugged. "I don't have anything else to give you, but we're gonna have exams soon," he said. "Like, in two weeks."

That meant just before her presentation.

"Oh, and Dr. Peterson wanted me to tell you that the grinder is dirty, as is the fecal sample blender," he said, with something like smugness. "So, if you have time in your busy schedule, you'll need to get that done."

Ani stared at Jeffrey's smirk until he shut the door. Then the pen that she held in her hand snapped, spilling red ink over her.

"God *damn* it," she yelled, quickly wiping off what she could and going down the hall to wash. She looked at herself in the mirror. She wasn't wearing makeup, and she looked exhausted. There was red all over her hands, and a bit on her neck, her cheek, her shirt.

Today sucked, she thought, as she went back to the office. She knew what was happening. Dr. Peterson was deliberately sabotaging her. He didn't believe women belonged in the lab, probably thought they were distracting or unqualified to do serious research. So, he was trying to guarantee the F... prevent her from having the time to do the presentation justice, and then he'd scrub her out.

She felt exhaustion creep up on her, and tears stung at her eyes. No. She wasn't going to let some sexist old fucker stop her from achieving her dream. She could work harder than he'd ever imagined. And he'd never know what hit him...

But God, I'm tired, she thought.

Her phone buzzed, and she checked it, wondering if it were Tessa. Instead, it was Abraham.

Abraham: Hey. YT?

She thought about ignoring it, since Abraham made her feel even more confused about her life. But she found herself typing back.

Ani: Yeah. What's up?

Abraham: Thought I'd bring you dinner. See you tonight.

Ani sighed. It sounded good, but it wouldn't do. She was starting to get addicted to him stopping by... not because he was eye candy, although he was. But because he was supportive, or seemed to be. Sure, it was probably because he wanted to get into her pants...

Or get into a relationship with her, for whatever reason.

What the hell, she thought. Maybe him getting into her pants wouldn't be a bad thing. Maybe that was the easiest way to keep it purely physical and not emotionally complicated. It'd be... a cork popping, just like Tessa had once said. She just needed a pressure release. She hated feeling so helpless, hated feeling like she was going to cry. She needed to get her groove back.

Ani: Sure. Why don't you bring it by my place tonight? I'm hungry for whatever you're bringing.

If that wasn't an invitation, she didn't know what was. And if she needed to... well, she could spell it out more clearly that night.

・♥ ・ ♥ ・ ♥ ・ ♥ ・ ♥ ・

Tonight was the night. He'd talked about waiting, but what the hell for? Ani was inviting him over, and it was clear from her text that she was in the mood. He hated to admit it, but maybe Dennis was right: he just needed to man up and get the job done.

Not that Ani was work of any sort. She was one of the least dramatic women he knew. Well, the rest of the bookstore crew, as well. He liked Kyla, and Tessa was quickly becoming one of his best friends. But Ani was special.

Stop that. Get out of your head.

The bottom line was, if he was going to have a relationship with Ani, and he was sure that was what he wanted, then he needed to make a stronger move. Their sex was off the charts, even she couldn't deny that. So he'd just seduce the hell out of her, and then they'd go from there.

He headed over to Ani's with determination. He felt his stomach knot slightly with tension. He wasn't nervous. It just reminded him of how he felt before game time — a mix of adrenaline and excitement. He didn't know how else to put it.

It was game time, and he was a go.

He knocked on her door, and she opened it. He felt his tongue thicken in his mouth.

"Hey," he said, taking her in. Her black hair was glossy and still damp from a shower, looking like an inky river with the slight waves that curled through it. She was wearing a tank top and a pair of shorty pajamas.

"Come in," she said, gesturing to him, all but grabbing him by the shirt and hauling him inside. "Let's do this."

"What do..."

Before he could say another word, she was on him, kissing him frantically. Their teeth clinked softly, and he couldn't help himself, he laughed. "Eager, huh?" he said.

She was five foot ten, easily — not exactly tiny. But he was six foot three, and built like a boulder where she was built like a sapling. She tangled herself around him like a vine, her arms curving around the back of his throat, giving her leverage. She leaped a little, wrapping her legs around his waist. He felt his body spring to attention.

"Bedroom?" he said. He'd meant to make things last a little longer, but if she was all for it, he was going to go with the flow. They could do slow and sexy the next round, he thought. It had been weeks since he'd been inside this woman, and damn it, he wanted to feel that incredible sensation again.

She nodded toward a door, and he opened it. There was laundry on the floor, he noticed, and the bed was unmade. There were books and papers on the bed, as well. "Are any of those important?"

"Oh, shit." She disengaged from him, quickly gathering up the papers and stuff. Then she looked around and saw that there wasn't much empty floor. An equally crowded chair, presumably with clean clothes, was mounded nearby. "Give me a sec."

"No problem," he said. He watched as she walked out to the living room. There was a small office desk against one wall. The kitchen table was mounded high with papers and textbooks. The walls had giant Post-it Notes and a whiteboard. The desk was littered with notebooks. There were dishes piled in the sink, he noticed, and the trash overflowed with takeout boxes. He remembered this from last time, the week or two ago when she'd said she wanted a wife.

When he turned to her, her bronze cheeks were a deep, dusky red with embarrassment. "I've been too busy to clean," she said, and he could hear the self-consciousness in every syllable. "I don't normally live like a slob."

"I wasn't judging you," he said, and meant it. "For God's sake, I hang out with Fezza, and he's almost set his place on fire. Twice. You cannot possibly be worse."

She smiled softly. "Well, as long as the bar's set low," she joked, then tugged him by the hand and crawled up on the bed. He stroked her ass, then followed the graceful curve of her hip and her back. She spread herself out on the bedding, arching like a cat, presenting her breasts for him like a buffet.

"Oh, yes," he breathed, leaning down and sucking first one, then the other through the thin T-shirt material. She wasn't wearing a bra! Hallelujah, he thought, sucking harder.

She gasped, writhing against him, her thighs rubbing against him. His cock went hard in a rush. He'd get her ready for him with an appetizer, he thought, then really rock her world, and his own, when they got to the main course.

He thought about the "feast" they'd had at the Erotic City convention. *Ain't got nothing on us*, he thought with a grin, as he tugged her pajama shorts off. No underwear under there, either, he noted with gratitude. She'd been prepared. Hell, yes, she wanted this.

He wanted this, too.

He tugged his shirt off, then pulled her tank top off, leaving her nude on the bed, looking like a mahogany sculpture. She was unspeakably beautiful, unconsciously graceful. He went back to how he'd first felt about her, at the con. She was like a goddess.

My goddess. He smiled hungrily.

Then he went back to touching her, his mouth devouring every inch of her, starting with her mouth. They exchanged carnivorous kisses, vicious in their intensity, until they pulled apart to breathe. He moved from there to the juncture of her throat and her collarbone, sucking hard enough to leave a mark. Her gasp and the way she wove her fingers into his hair told him she liked that maneuver. He stroked the mark with his tongue before moving lower, tracing a pattern to her still pebbled nipples, taking her perfectly curved breasts into his mouth one at a time.

He headed lower, dipping into her belly button, then parting her legs and stroking her slippery seam. She gasped again, then let out soft, panting breaths as her hips levered up to meet him. He obliged her, leaning down and licking her soft folds. She jerked against him, but he held her hips taut while he went to town, savoring the tangy taste of her, reveling in the feel of her hard clit under its fleshy hood.

She was gasping hard now, wriggling against him, her thighs gripping him on either side of his face, and he kept delving, adding his fingers to press inside her wetness. He reached up, searching for her spot, and loved the sound she made when he found it.

"*Abraham*," she almost shrieked, shivering uncontrollably.

He smiled against her, then redoubled his efforts. By God, this was going to knock her out.

She was breathing hard, her hips pistoning as best they could under his grip, her hands grasping the sheets like she was trying to find some way to tether herself to the bed. He kept up his relentless assault until he heard her breathing go fast and choppy and her noises grow more helplessly desperate.

"Abraham... oh, baby, I'm gonna... I'm coming... oh God, I'm coming..."

He sucked her clit into his mouth, swirling around the hard button with the flat of his tongue as his fingers plunged inside her. With a low scream of pleasure, she shuddered against him, flooding his mouth with her taste. He felt the walls of her shudder and clench around his hands, and his cock jerked in response, so hard it was painful.

After long moments, he pressed a gentle kiss against her, leaning up on his forearm and removing his fingers from her. She was lying there, still as a carved angel. "Ready for round two?" he said, reaching for his zipper.

She made a low noise, like "Mmmm." He frowned. Normally she was louder. Maybe she was making him work for it. He liked that idea.

Then he heard a low, ladylike snore.

He blinked. "Ani?" Then he shook her lightly. "Ani? Are you... *asleep?*"

There was the tiniest, cutest snort. Then she shifted to her side, snuggling into the pillow.

He was shocked. He'd rocked her world, all right. And now... now, she was *asleep!*

He was torn between being embarrassed, being irritated, and being amused. It was funny, since the guy was usually the one that hit it and fell asleep. But his cock was ready to roll, and it found the whole situation less funny. Beyond that, it was hard to think "this is a relationship, not a booty call" when your partner dropped out after she got hers.

He was thinking all that when he finally really looked at her. She had smudges under her eyes. Exhaustion. Maybe she'd even been crying.

She'd been tired. She was now pushing into burn-out. What had she said? She had a hard time getting in the mood when her place was a mess. He'd seen this in programmers, when their cubicles turned into disaster zones during deadline crunch. She was starting to crack up.

Well, he'd helped with one form of stress relief, he thought, getting up gingerly and adjusting his still-sore cock, which was gradually and sullenly shrinking back to normal. He could help her with another, because while she might be wiped out, he got the feeling it'd be a while before he got any sleep.

A little investigation revealed an in-unit washer-dryer. He got a load of laundry started, then unloaded the dishwasher as best he could before clearing the dirty dishes and starting that up. He took several trips to the trash chute until all the garbage was gone, then even went ahead and cleaned the bathroom. He didn't touch any of the papers or books — he figured she had some kind of system going, and he didn't want to mess with it.

He wasn't any kind of housekeeper, but the place did seem a little nicer when he was done. He hoped that she felt that way, too. *When she wakes up,* he thought with a grin.

Then he waited.

By ten o'clock, he'd realized that she was asleep for the long haul. *So much for a booty call,* he thought, his body still achy and longing. He really shouldn't make a production out of it. He went into the darkened bedroom, kissing her. "I'm gonna go, Ani," he said against her jawline.

"No," she said, wrapping her bare arms around him. "No, stay. I'll wake up in a minute."

"You're not gonna wake up until the morning," he countered.

She held him tighter, biting his earlobe. "Then stay until then," she breathed.

His cock stood at attention, and he groaned. "Girl, you do *not* play fair."

She sighed as she snuggled back into bed. He got himself ready, then kept his boxers on and climbed in next to her. He gritted his teeth as she snuggled up against him. He smelled her shampoo — something tropical, like coconut maybe? — and sighed as he felt her whisper soft skin brushing up against his own.

"I really like you, Ani," he said against the crown of her head. "You make me crazy, but damned if I don't like you."

She made a little incoherent sound of happiness and cuddled harder. This was not how he'd planned this evening to go, he thought. But he couldn't help but feel a warm sense of contentment, one he hadn't felt in years, if ever. With that, he snuggled against her and, sooner than he would've thought, he fell asleep.

CHAPTER 8

Ani woke up feeling weird. It took her a second to realize it was feeling rested. Then she turned over and squelched a yelp.

There was a man in her bed. He had his back to her, his copper hair tousled and....

Wait.

Copper hair?

She ran her hand through her hair, her memory scrambling. She remembered inviting Abraham over. She remembered doing it with the express purpose of blowing off some steam, just getting laid and seeing if that would help her improve her outlook on life, because she was feeling like shit. But then he'd come over, and...

Blank.

Jeez, Louise, she'd been unbelievably tired. But she'd never slept through sex before, and she couldn't believe she'd sleep through sex with Abraham. What had happened?

She hopped out of bed, noticing that she was naked. That... was problematic, she thought. Gah, gah, gah.

She threw on a pair of pants, headed to the bathroom and brushed her teeth, then ran a brush through her hair. What was she going to do? Did she ask him what happened that night? She frowned as her brush hit a snarl.

Stay, she'd asked. *Stay, and we can do something after I get some rest.*

He'd stayed all night. Holy crap.

She walked out of the bathroom, then stopped dead as she saw the kitchen.

She'd been running out of dishes. He'd loaded the dishwasher for her, which meant that he must've unloaded the dishwasher, too, at some point. She'd probably be finding her stuff in weird places, but the thoughtfulness of the gesture warmed her chest in a way she hadn't felt in years. Had a boyfriend ever noticed that the dishes were dirty, much less decided to clean?

Maybe he was OCD, she argued with herself weakly, trying to keep her defenses up. He was ex-military, after all. Keeping things clean and orderly was probably his jam.

She saw that there was also a basket of clean laundry, and another load in the dryer. Even as she felt embarrassed that her house had been in that condition... he'd taken care of her.

And holy cow, she must've been exhausted if he'd done all this and she'd slept through it. She wondered what he'd looked like while he was doing it.

"Morning," he said.

She looked away from the laundry and the kitchen to find him shirtless in just jeans. Her mouth went dry. It ought to be illegal for a man to look that damned good in the morning. Or ever.

"I'm just gonna..." He gestured to the bathroom.

"Huh? Oh! Sure, yeah, of course." She nodded, feeling like an idiot. Then she glanced at the clock. "Oh! Oh, shit. It's nine!"

"You late for something?" he said through the closed door.

"Yes! Wait. What day is it?" She looked at a calendar. "Oh, thank God. Saturday."

"Can you take the day off?" She heard water running. "'Cause it seems like you definitely need the rest."

"No rest for the wicked. Or grad students," she said with a weak laugh. "I'm gonna need to log some more time in the lab today definitely."

"You have time for a..."

Before he could ask, there was a knock on the door. She jumped, letting out a little startled squeal. She looked through the peephole.

"Oh, shit! It's Tessa," Ani said.

"So?" He emerged. His gray eyes were bright.

"Get in the bedroom and don't come out, okay? Just... just don't make a sound." She started shoving him, but he was an immovable, wall-like mass.

"You ashamed of me?" He sounded like he was teasing, but she did hear a note of hurt beneath it.

"I don't want to explain this! Worlds colliding, worlds colliding!" she said. "Just... keep it quiet, okay?"

She shoved him the rest of the way in, closing the door. Then she opened the front door. Tessa had a box of Steve's Donuts, the best donuts in Snoqualmie, with several Bavarian creams — Ani's favorite.

"I'm sorry I haven't been able to help more," Tessa said, without preamble. "I've been so busy with the game, I've been running a little ragged."

"It's not your responsibility to take care of me," Ani said. "I'm sorry I can't help *you* more."

"Oh, it's no problem," Tessa said with a dismissive wave of her hand. "I've got Adam. He's been working on project managing, but he's also been cooking every day of the week and doing laundry. He even gives me back rubs and massages when I'm stressed." She giggled. "Of course, those tend to turn into other things."

Ani wiggled her eyebrows. "Best kind of stress relief, huh?"

"I'm telling you, having a boyfriend is the best," Tessa said. Then she looked aghast. "Being single's good, too. Probably better than being with the wrong guy."

Ani felt guilt, her eyes shifting to the closed bedroom door. "Um... speaking of stress relief..."

Tessa followed the direction of her gaze, and her jaw dropped. "No. *Way*!" she whispered. "Who is he?"

"Um..." Ani shook her head. "Remember how I told you I hooked up with a guy at Erotic City?"

Tessa's eyes widened. "You tracked him down again?"

"I kept his contact info," Ani said carefully. "And... well, he was really good, so..."

Tessa's smile was like the sun. "So, did you have a good time?"

She thought about saying "I fell asleep" but just couldn't bring herself to. "Um... yeah," she said.

"I won't take up more of your time, but... how is it?" Tessa asked, with a giggle.

Ani smiled. "He's not like anybody else I know," she said honestly.

"Do you think it could turn into a relationship?"

Ani paused. "I doubt it," she said.

Tessa studied her. "But you're thinking about it," she said. "I know you. I know that look on your face. You really like this guy."

Ani prayed that he wasn't listening, and she glared at her friend. Tessa blinked. "He's awake?" she mouthed.

Ani nodded frantically, and Tessa reddened.

"Sorry," she mouthed again, then cleared her throat. "Well, I'll just leave these donuts with you and get going," she said with a grin. "Call me later, okay?"

"Okay," Ani said, giving Tessa a big hug and whispering in her ear, "I'll tell you everything later," she said, promising herself that she'd come clean about Abraham.

Tessa hustled away. Abraham came out, leaning against the doorframe.

"Want me to be your boyfriend, huh?" he said.

"I have to go to the lab," she said, feeling her cheeks redden. "And I didn't say I want you to be anything. I know that's not your jam. You just want to hit it and quit it."

"That's true," he said.

She felt her stomach drop unpleasantly.

"At least, it was true," he said, his voice lowering until she shivered like someone had rubbed her naked body with a mink glove. "Now, I just know I want to see you. I want to be with you."

She nodded. "I'll be working late tonight," she said quietly. "I have to do an experiment in the lab most of the day tomorrow. My life from here on out is really, really busy."

She could feel his disappointment. Hell, she could feel her own.

Then she heard herself speak. "But... yeah," she agreed tentatively. "This week, maybe we can, you know. Talk about it. See where it can go."

He smiled. "I'd like that."

Then he scooped her up, carrying her to the bedroom. She yelped. "What are you doing?"

"You promised when you were rested we'd finish what we started," he said, and she burst into laughter.

· ♥ · ♥ · ♥ · ♥ · ♥ ·

"What's going on, Abraham? You level up on some hard-core mode or something?" Fezza asked.

Abraham absently looked up from the coding he'd been doing. "Huh?"

"You've had this smile on your face for the past, like, two hours," Fezza said.

"I have?" Abraham rubbed a hand over his jaw. Sure enough, what felt like a shit-eating grin was stretching his face. He tried to force his scowl. "So what?"

"So you never smile like that," Fezza said, "and frankly, it's freaking some of the guys out."

Abraham's snicker was evil. "As they should be."

"Oh, shit." Fezza's eyes wheeled. "You're not making us do a coding boot camp, are you? Because they are heinous."

"Maybe."

"Or... no, we're not in crunch time. We're not doing some team-building exercise, are we?" Fezza's voice got higher-pitched. "Because the last time you had us do paintball guns, I was bruised for a month, I swear."

Abraham thought of torturing him more, then just shrugged. He was in too good a mood. "Nah, we're not doing either. I'm just having a good day."

"Really?" Fezza said.

"Is it that surprising?"

Fezza sent him a narrowed side-eye stare. "Whatever," he finally admitted, then retreated to his own cubicle.

Abraham hadn't seen Ani since his wake-up call with her on Saturday morning. She'd been busy with grading and lab work, but he was going to stop by tonight. He was going to angle to stay, too, if possible. Even though they'd managed to have sex before she'd gone out Saturday, he found himself craving her. There was anticipation, excitement, a sense of...

Joy, he thought. He was happier than he could remember with this weird-ass... whatever it was they had.

Relationship.

She hadn't said as much, but he was working her around to the idea, he just knew it. She hadn't told Tessa, but he hadn't told his guys, either, and honestly didn't know when he planned to.

A secret relationship was still a relationship, though, right?

Puzzled, distracted, he got up to check on the other architects, seeing their progress on various games. He checked on Jose, then he went over to Tessa to see how she was doing on her new project.

"How's it going?"

Tessa pulled herself up proudly, gesturing to the lines of code and the documents. "On time, on budget," she said proudly. "And we hit all our OKRs this past week."

He nodded, impressed. OKRs — objectives and key results — were the beating heart of any dev team, and the fact that she took them seriously was a good sign. "You're a good programmer," he said. "You're going to be a great game developer."

She was grinning like a madwoman when she winced, rubbing at her shoulder and neck. "Been pushing myself a little hard lately," she said with a rueful grin.

He grinned back, remembering what he'd overheard at Ani's. "What, Adam falling down on his masseur duties?"

Tessa's eyes widened like he'd smacked her, and suddenly he remembered. He'd overheard it while he was *hiding* at Ani's.

Shit.

"Adam didn't tell you that, did he?" she said quietly. "Because he wouldn't talk about it with the guys — you all make fun of him enough." She dropped her voice even lower. "Been to any conventions lately, boss?"

They were still in the pit, in the room, so the other guys could hear them, even if they didn't know what they were talking about. "Yeah, we hit Erotic City," Dennis said. "Abraham here even hit it with some freak."

Tessa's eyes went wide.

"I think he's still bumpin' boots with her," Dennis said. "Why else would he be so happy? I'll bet he..."

"Dennis, shut the fuck up."

You could've heard a bubble break in the charged silence that followed. "What?" Dennis said, then lowered his voice at Jose's shove. "What?"

Tessa headed out, and Abraham waited a beat before following her upstairs to the break room. She was making herself hot chocolate, but he could tell by her jerky movements that she was none too pleased with him.

"You're involved with Ani?"

"I don't see how that's your business."

"She's my best friend," Tessa said, her voice sharp. "I worry about her."

"She didn't tell you about me." He still wasn't sure how he felt about that, either. "If she wanted you to worry about this, don't you think she would've said something?"

"She knows I'm working on this project. Maybe she's trying not to stress me out."

"Maybe she felt like it wasn't your business, either," he said, then softened the blow when he saw Tessa's brown eyes spark. "Or maybe she just didn't think it was that big a deal."

Which he knew was a lie. It was a big deal. He couldn't believe how big it felt, honestly.

Tessa seemed to think about that for a second, then let out a low exhalation. "I know that she's a grown woman, and you're right, it's not my business." She stirred the cocoa. "But I will say this: if you hurt her, I will make your life very unpleasant. All the girls will."

"What, you gonna borrow Kyla's tasers?" he tried to joke.

"I'll do something," Tessa said, "because Ani's my best friend in the whole world. I love her. And I won't let some guy who doesn't care about her jerk her around and hurt her, okay?"

"What if she's jerking me around?" he said before he could stop himself. "Maybe she's just using me. Ever thought of that?"

She blinked. Then she smiled sadly.

"If she was like that," Tessa said, "do you really think you would have been there at her apartment two weeks later?"

She walked away, leaving him to sit and think about what she said. In the old days, the news would have panicked him: Ani was a clinger. She wanted a relationship. He was jumping through hoops and she'd expect him to stay around.

But he didn't feel panic. If anything, he felt... that contentment, that happiness, bubbling to the surface.

Now, he just had to pray that Tessa was right: that Ani was invested. And he was going to keep her that way.

· ♥ · ♥ · ♥ · ♥ · ♥ ·

Another week down. Another week where she'd barely had time to work on her proposal defense, she thought.

"Finally," Ani said with a sigh as the last set of experiments were completed for the day. All her chores were taken care of, all the grading (and re-grading) was finished. She felt like a fairy-tale princess who had finally gotten the long list of chores from the evil stepmother done. She couldn't believe it.

Abraham was supposed to see her, bring by dinner with the idea of maybe spending a bit more time together. This was still confusing for her, but she knew that he'd been persistent, and she was tired of holding out, especially when he was being so supportive. If he was just in it for the sex, would he really have done the dishes and taken out the trash and done her laundry? Brought her something to eat in the lab or the TA room almost every night? Was he just pretending to be a nice guy, lulling her into a false confidence so she'd give it up? He didn't seem the type, and it wasn't like she was putting up huge barriers. He could get sex from just about anywhere. Why would he wait? He'd already had her, as it were. And yeah, she'd thought the sex was off the charts. But would he just stay in it for the sex, do all this just to have another go at her?

Did he really want a relationship?

And how long would he want to keep going?

"Hey Ani," Jeffrey's voice chimed in, too cheerful. "Did you finish that grading?"

Startled out of her reverie, she stared at Jeffrey for a second.

"I didn't mean to interrupt your daydreaming," he said, sarcasm evident. "But Dr. Peterson wanted me to check on your progress."

"I finished everything," she said, keeping her voice casual even as she felt the desire to clench her teeth. "I was just going to pack up for the day."

"Really?" One of his blond eyebrows went up, and he checked a list he was holding. "You finished cleaning out the oil pump?"

"Yes."

"The equipment..."

"Cleaned the autoclave" — again, she thought with resentment — "the blender, the glassware."

"The experiments he asked..."

"Done." She knew she shouldn't be cutting him off, because he'd no doubt express her rudeness to Dr. Peterson, but she couldn't help but feel a bubble of pride and, yeah, smugness.

He pursed his lips. "Well. I suppose you're done for the night, then," he said, with an offhand gesture. Like he was her boss or something, not a fellow teaching assistant. She gritted her teeth.

"He doesn't have any other experiments for me," she said. "I've got everything checked off, and the grading's complete. As is the re-grading."

He glowered at her. "If it had been done properly the first time, Dr. Peterson wouldn't have had to issue that edict, I'm sure."

She wanted to glower back at him, since it had been just as she expected: a waste of time. The stuff she regraded had wound up exactly as it had been the first time. Still, she knew that she only had a few weeks to her proposal.

"I am spending the weekend working on my proposal," she said.

"Ah, yes. About that." He looked at his list again. "Dr. Peterson said that he'd been trying to reach you but hadn't been able to. The board's had to change schedule, so they've moved your proposal defense ahead by two weeks."

Her jaw dropped. "*Two weeks*? That's only two weeks away!"

"You should be far enough along that this doesn't present a hardship," Jeffrey said, although she swore she saw him flush. Obviously Dr. Peterson was having Jeffrey be the fall guy on this shitty announcement, and even if Jeffrey liked having someone else do his grading, this kind of hatchet job was unfair and unpleasant. "Dr. Peterson said most people in your position would be done. This was a decision by the advisory board. If you have problems, you could bring it up with them — although Dr. Peterson mentioned that he didn't know whether they would think that your pursuing this avenue of research is a good idea if you do."

She felt tears pricking at her eyes. She wanted to scream.

Dr. Peterson had pulled this off, somehow. What she'd suspected, she now knew for a fact. He'd done passive interference, throwing crap work her way, doing the re-grading, taking up as much time as possible with stupid experiments that he didn't really need. Now he was actively on the offensive. He was trying to boot her out of the program.

"You're not going to cry, are you?" He said, his voice tinged with distaste. "I honestly hate it when women cry, and they seem to do it all the time. It's not appropriate. This isn't personal, it's simply science. Crying and getting emotional is not going to sway my decision, and it doesn't change anything." He cleared his throat. "Also, um, Dr. Peterson told me to tell him if you did."

She'd rip her own arms off before she let him see her cry, she thought, willing herself to keep the tears at bay.

There was a knock, and the door to the lab opened. "Hey, I brought that pad Thai with fried tofu you like," Abraham said without preamble, then stopped in his tracks, taking in the scene in front of him. "Sorry. I didn't mean to interrupt."

He'd been bringing by food the past week, not staying long, not doing anything inappropriate — as in, not making her come on a countertop or destroying anything expensive. But he'd sent her some smoldering looks, and kissed her into oblivion, before simply walking away and leaving her to her work. It was stuff that had kept her up late and reduced the battery life in her vibrator when she got home. It was as if he were proving to her that he was here for the long term. Other than teasing her about falling asleep after sex "just like a guy" he'd been caring, supportive, and basically perfect.

Jeffrey's expression was derisive. "Are you supposed to be here?" Then he looked at Ani. "Is this someone you know? Or is he just a delivery boy?"

Abraham drew himself up to his full six foot three. The delivery boy comment was going over well, obviously.

"I'm here to see my girl," Abraham said, his tone cold. "And bring her dinner."

"Your *girl*." Jeffrey looked at Ani. "Strangers and non-students are not allowed in the lab."

"He brings me dinner," she said. "And there's no policy that specifically...."

"I shouldn't be surprised that you're breaking rules," Jeffrey said with disgust.

She tilted her head and studied Jeffrey for a second. His tone was a little...

Oh shit. He can't be jealous.

She sighed. It never occurred to her that Jeffrey had a thing for her, especially given his behavior. But now he was acting pissy. Like she needed another man aggravated with her and causing her problems.

"You can't stay," Jeffrey said sharply to Abraham. "Drop off your food and leave."

Abraham's expression was both amused and vicious as he leaned back against a counter, crossing his arms so the muscles bulged beneath the t-shirt. "Or what?"

Jeffrey goggled, his mouth working like a fish on a boat bottom. "What do you mean, or what?"

"If I hang out here while she's eating, what's going to happen to me? And who's going to enforce that?" He gave Jeffrey a once-over. "You gonna throw down with me, Pipe Cleaner?"

Now Jeffrey backed up and hit the counter. She all but dragged Abraham out of the lab. "Who was that asshole?" Abraham said. "And why was he treating you like shit, and calling me stupid? I'm ready to beat some fucking manners into that guy."

"Don't," she said quickly, dropping her voice. "He's Dr. Peterson's favorite, and they'll just find some way to turn it back on me anyway."

"This is all such bullshit," Abraham pointed out, sounding incensed. "This Peterson guy gives you all this shit work, while his favorite gets to dump his grading on you. Tell me this isn't just some way of keeping you from doing your own stuff."

She blinked. She'd complained a little about her position, just blowing off steam while she ate and while Abraham hung out. But she hadn't realized he'd been listening and retaining it.

"I will say this: he's right. Long hours, stupid experiments, repetitious stuff... that can be grad school," she said, with a sigh. "It's not all exciting research and new discoveries. There's a lot of bonehead stuff. But it is what it is."

Abraham still looked mulish. "You're not coming in to work tomorrow, are you?"

"No," she said. "And thank God. I have to work on my proposal defense. That... " She bit back on the term *dickhead*, since he might still be lurking the hallways, "... *guy* just told me that my proposal is due two weeks earlier than I expected. I'm pretty far along, but I wanted to make sure it was perfect, so this weekend will be focused on that."

"Do you have to work on it tonight?" He said. " Or can you take a break?"

She thought about it. She ought to work on it. She really should. But between the confrontation with Jeffrey, she felt like her shoulder blades were fused together. Her brain felt like mush and her muscles were ready to explode. She needed the stress relief.

Oh, just be honest. It's not just sex. You want to spend time with Abraham. And that was a dangerous realization.

"I could take tonight," she admitted softly. "Off, I mean."

He stood straighter. "Let's eat this at my place, then."

There was a moment of silence as the invitation sat there. She thought about it. She didn't know what this meant in their relationship — if they had one. If it would change things. She didn't know.

But right now, she didn't care.

"Okay," she said. "You drive, I'll follow you in my car."

CHAPTER 9

Abraham was feeling a combination of anxious and excited when he headed back to his house with the Thai take-out on the front seat. It seemed like he was forever feeding the girl who still looked like a willow no matter how much food she chowed down on. She probably worried it off, he thought with a grin. The grin faded as he thought about the exchange with that blond guy, Jeffrey. Of course, with the assholes in her life, especially the ones gunning for her career, she did have a lot to worry about.

He wished he could've smacked the smug out of that fucker. But she was right: they would've found some way to make her pay for it, and he was doing everything he could to make her life easier at this point.

He shook his head at himself. He was acting like a chick, he thought, then thought of Tessa's dressing-down. Yeah, that was sexist. But he certainly wasn't acting like the manly figure his father had emphasized and the military had codified. He didn't just want to be Ani's booty call and stress relief. She was smart. She was fun. Yeah, she was sexy as hell, but she was also loyal and brilliant and didn't take his shit. She wasn't cowed by him, and he had grown men who were skittish around him. He respected the hell out of Ani, and he wanted to see how far they could go.

Other than his admittedly dysfunctional relationships in the past, where his girlfriends cheated on him or started drama and insisted on grand displays or crazy hysterics, Ani had her own life, one that didn't rely on causing explosions and then picking up the pieces. Ani didn't have time for that shit, nor would she be interested if she did have time. Ani was what he should've been looking for all along.

So he wasn't going to let her just leap on him tonight.

His body protested immediately. *Hey! We like leaping!*

All right, he allowed. He wasn't just going to let her leap on him right from the jump. They were going to have a talk first, maybe over the food. He wanted to find out where she thought their relationship was going. It had hurt, the first time they were together, for her to say that she was ashamed of being with him. His father had pointed out that women like her never thought that guys like him were good enough. Was she still ashamed of him? Did she still feel that way?

His parked his car in his driveway and grabbed the take-out bag as Ani parked behind him. God damn it. Was he setting himself up to fail?

Too late now, he thought, as Ani walked up to him.

"You know, I've never seen your house," she said. She was wearing a T-shirt that was a swirl of yellow and orange and a pair of jeans, her hair in a French braid. He'd been so pissed at Jeffrey and the whole situation at the lab he hadn't even paid attention to her. That, he thought, was stupid.

"You look beautiful," he said, then winced. He meant it, but damn it, he usually had more finesse than this. And he didn't usually sound like such a dork.

Still, the comment surprised her and must've pleased her, since she blushed a little.

He unlocked the front door, then brought her inside, looking it over. He hadn't expected company, so he was glad that it wasn't a complete mess. He looked at it with fresh eyes, imagining what she might be feeling. He had a gaming chair and his gaming computer out on a desk, as well as his console and his big screen TV with surround sound. There was also the big micro-suede sofa with a stain from when Fezza had dropped soda on it. The dining table was clear, at least.

"I love Arts and Crafts bungalows," she breathed, looking around, her fingers tracing the molding along the doors and the chair rail. "You own this place?"

He nodded.

She smiled at him. "You're such a grown-up."

He smiled back. "You hungry?"

"You don't have to keep bringing me take-out, you know," she said, as he put the food down on the dining room table. "I feel badly."

"It's a habit now," he said, walking in and handing the bag to her as he closed the door. "Besides, I like feeding you." *I like providing for you*, his brain supplied. He squelched a sigh at himself.

Her eyes were hungry, but the hunger had nothing to do with food, since she made no move for the take-out bags. Her gaze traced over him, lingering. "Did I ever tell you about the 'sensual feast'? The one at Erotic City?" she said. "It was mostly silly, but there were a few inventive ideas that I wouldn't mind trying with you."

All his blood rushed down south to second brain, and he swallowed hard. "Oh?" he said, his voice strangled to his own ears.

"Yeah." She started to tug him to the bedroom. "But let's start with an appetizer, get our..."

"Whoa. Wait," he said, determined, even though his brain was screaming at him for his stupidity. "I want to know: what are we doing here?"

She blinked. "We're... seriously? You don't know?"

"No. I mean, I know what we're about to do," he said, rolling his eyes. "But is that all this is? Is it just sex?"

She pulled away, and he felt it like an ice wall between them. "I'm sorry. Are you asking what my intentions are?"

He crossed his arms, even as his cock felt like a lead pipe in his jeans. "I guess I am. I mean, I don't mind being a booty call, but... well, shit. With you, I do."

"You do what?"

"Mind being a booty call," he said. "You're smart, and awesome, and hotter than hell. And I want to know I'm more than just some guy that you call up for a quick stress break."

She sighed. "I don't know."

His eyes widened. "You don't know?"

She bit her lip. "I really like you. More than I expected to," she said.

He felt his stomach turn to ice, and his cock flagged a bit. "Thanks," he drawled, the sting of her words slapping at him.

"No." She walked over to him, stroking his face with her hand, and he forced himself not to pull away. "I mean, I started caring about you despite not wanting to. You're not my usual type, at all."

"You're not my usual type, either."

"And despite my initial impressions of you — I guess that's not a bad thing."

He frowned, unsure of what she meant.

"You're grumpy, and you still have some toxic masculinity issues," she said. "But you also put yourself out for me. You bring me food, you give me support, without making expectations or anything as a result. You want to be seen as more. You're not what I expected."

"You're not what I expected, either," he grumbled.

"I care about you," she repeated. "And I know I'm not in a good place right now. All my energy, all my focus, is on getting through this proposal defense. I just want to prove to myself and to my family that I can do this, you know? Does that make sense? Until that's done, I don't think I can focus on anything else. So can we make a more permanent decision after that?"

"No," he said, nudging her. "If I did that to you, if I said that I had something else that was more important, and could we put what we've got on the table until... I don't know, until my game was done or something, you'd kick my ass. And you'd be right to. Because that's not how relationships work."

She looked down, then took a deep breath. "You're right," she whispered. "If you did, I'd kick your ass."

He couldn't help himself. He grinned. "So, what are we doing here?"

She waited an interminably long minute, and he felt himself slowly going mad.

Then she spoke.

"I... I guess I'm all in on this," she said, nodding slowly. "But please — please, don't hurt me, okay? Because this scares the hell out of me."

"Believe it or not, it scares the hell out of me, too," he admitted, then swept her up into his arms and headed for the bedroom. "But let's be scared together."

· ♥ · ♥ · ♥ · ♥ · ♥ ·

She felt light-headed as Abraham carried her from the living room to the bedroom. She'd been so careful to keep him a secret from the people she cared about. Maybe that was unfair of her. Her parents would grill her mercilessly about him. Tessa would be shocked about him, more than likely; she might like him as a boss, now that he'd finally seen her abilities, but at the same time, Tessa knew about his chauvinistic tendencies.

Ani knew that she could be attracted to Alpha-holes. Was this what this was?

Abraham stretched her out on the bed, taking off his shirt and temporarily short-circuiting her brain. "You're thinking too much," he pointed out, his copper beard stretching over his wide grin. "It's all right, baby. I'm going to take care of you."

Baby. She liked the endearment, even though she didn't generally. "I can take care of myself," she said, just because the idea was so weird for her.

He took off his pants next, and she saw him in all his naked glory – those muscles, and good God, that happy trail of reddish brown that led to one of the most magnificent cocks she'd ever had the pleasure of experiencing.

"I like doing things for you," he rumbled. "And I know how hard it is for you to let me. But let me, baby. Please?"

Oh, *gah*. This guy made her brain leak out of her ears. Did she stand a chance against him?

She reached down, pulling up the hemline of her T-shirt and whipping it over her head, leaving her in only a salmon-colored bra.

She saw the moment his pupils dilated, and his breathing went short.

"You are so insanely beautiful," he said, and just like when he'd said it before, she shivered. Probably the way he said it, almost reverently, not a glib ploy to get her into bed. He had to know they were headed there anyway. Nothing was going to stop her from having him now, or stop her from giving herself over to the pleasure she knew he could provide for her.

He reached down, slipping her jeans off of her legs, leaving her only in underwear. Then he stretched out on top of her, his cock teasing at her panties, his mouth moving between her breasts, his beard tickling at the edges of her bra. She arched a little, encouraging him, then sighing heavily as he finally got the hint and took one cloth-covered nipple into his mouth. She angled one leg around him, his hardness coming into closer contact with her wetness as he sucked more intently, dampening the fabric around her breast with his searching tongue.

"Abraham," she moaned, her hips rolling and stroking him. His cock felt hard and hot and glorious against her, and she wanted more. "Please."

He chuckled against her skin, then reached behind her, undoing the clasp and removing the bra. He pulled back. "You're usually in a hurry, you know that?"

"I know what I want," she said.

He slipped his fingers in the waistband of her panties, slowly, torturously dragging them down her legs as her hips bucked slightly. "There is something to be said for going slow," he murmured.

"You're a guy," she said. "Never in the history of guy-dom has one ever said, 'I'd much rather go slow.' At least, not in my experience."

"Well, then, it's time you learned," he said, rubbing first one arch of her foot, then the other. Considering she'd been on her feet a lot lately at the lab, it felt like heaven, and all the sexy hormones that had been driving her like a whip slowed down slightly, savoring the sensation.

"You're going to make me fall asleep again," she warned him, even though there was a soft sigh of contentment in her voice.

He stopped, and she almost whimpered. "Well, we can't have that," he joked. Then he kissed her calf, then the pit behind her knee... her thigh. She braced herself for him moving to her pussy, but instead he backed off, kissing her other leg, trailing light licks towards her center.

"*Abraham*," she murmured frantically, her body writhing as he slowly built her up again. How could he be so patient, so goddamned forbearing, while she felt like she was going through a slow-building inferno?

"Hurry," she said, almost angry, until she saw that slow smile cross his face, one that made her stomach go fluttery, not just with sexual nerves, but with a feeling of... well, she wasn't sure *what* she was feeling.

He opened a drawer in the nightstand, pulling out a condom, putting it on. His eyes barely left hers. "Do you know why I'm going so slow with you?" he asked.

Unable to speak, she shook her head.

"Because this isn't just sex, Ani. We're in a relationship, okay? I'm not letting you treat this like some hit-it-and-quit-it, or pretend it is in your head. I don't know what we have, but it sure as hell isn't quick. Or temporary," he added.

She started trembling a little. "You don't 'let' me do anything," she said instead, even as she struggled not to be overwhelmed by the complicated morass of emotions swamping her.

He laughed, notching himself between her legs. "No, I don't," he said. "You are one of the most independent women I know. Which may be why I feel so much for you. Why I want you so badly. Why I... oh *God*."

With that, he slid in. She was wet enough that there was no friction, although he was large enough that the progress was still slow as she accommodated his size. She bit back a gasp.

"Baby," he breathed. "Oh, God, you feel so fucking good."

It was like a sexual tango, perfectly choreographed and sensual as hell. He leaned up on his arms, his hips moving to shift that cock of his inside her, stroking against her G-spot before retreating, circling slightly so her whole body shook and her clit got equal attention. He moved with deliberate precision and masterful grace, like an engineer crossed with an artist.

She clutched at his back as an orgasm blindsided her. She let out a yell, her body trembling. When she got her bearings again, his gray eyes were glittering, and his smile was broad.

"That's one."

"Oh, no. We're not doing a marathon. I will get hungry eventually," she said, smiling back at him. She nudged him. "Flip over. It's my turn to be in control."

"This isn't about control," he said, in that low, sexy-growly voice. "This is about... *ahhh, God.*"

She lowered herself onto his stiffness, doing a slow body roll of her own. She saw his eyes roll back in his head.

"What was that you were saying?" she inquired sweetly as she pulled up almost all the way, then slowly but firmly glided down the length of his erection.

He muttered something incoherent, his hands holding her hips, fingers digging in to pull her to him.

"Slow, right?" she asked, relishing the power she was feeling, and the ability to heighten the pleasure for both of them.

He grimaced. Then, to her surprise, he nodded, even though sweat was beading his brow.

"Because you are worth it," he ground out.

She stopped, then kissed him, deep as he was buried inside her. He laced his fingers in the hair at the nape of her neck, then lifted his hips to meet hers, lifting her off the bed.

"I think I'm falling in love with you, Abraham," she whispered against his mouth.

She pulled back enough to see him blink at her. Then she swiveled her hips, tripping her own spot, and feeling the slow beginnings of an orgasm start to build. She moved her hips faster, and she felt him starting to lose control beneath her. He sat up, clutching her to him. She wrapped her legs around him, and their bodies slapped together as he pierced her over and over.

She tilted her head back and cried out as the next orgasm hit her, more powerful than the first. She felt it echo yet again when his body shuddered, and he lost control, losing himself inside of the condom inside her.

After a long minute, he let go of her, giving her kisses along her jaw, down her neck, along her shoulder.

He didn't say anything about what she'd admitted, she noticed. But he was the one who was pushing for a relationship.

"You hungry?" he said finally. "Because even though it might not be a marathon, I think that later we'll probably be up for a few more laps."

She chuckled, but her stomach clenched a little. Had she gone too far, too fast?

Had she made a huge mistake?

Please don't be an asshole, she thought. *Please, please.... be as invested as I am.*

• ♥ • ♥ • ♥ • ♥ • ♥ •

It felt weird, but cool, to wake up with Ani in his bed.

They had breakfast. Using what he had around, he made her Denver omelets. While he missed bacon, it still felt awesome to have a meal with her, to watch her glowing and laughing as she talked and ate. Then they took a shower together, which was even more awesome, especially when they got to the part where she wrapped her legs around him and he had her against the cool tiles.

She needed to work on her proposal, and he knew that it was important enough that he had to be smart enough to let her go handle her business. "I wish you could stay," he said, knowing damned well that she couldn't. This was her career, and it was important, both to her, and honestly, to the world. What kind of a dick would he be if he kept her at his house so they could... what, watch movies or something? Have more sex?

"I wish I could stay too," she said, kissing him gently. "But I'm running out of time as it is."

"I know, I know," he agreed. He watched as she sighed, her dark brown eyes going even darker. "What's up?" he asked.

"I think I've got the proposal defense itself down, honestly. Even on a shorter timeline," she said. "But I've gone over it for so long, so many times, I think I'm losing perspective."

He nodded. "I know what that's like," he said. "After a certain point in a game, you wonder if you've got too much feature creep or if it's awesome or it really just sucks. Usually like a pendulum: it's awesome! it sucks! It's awesome! It sucks!"

She laughed, leaning up, and nodding. "That's it. Of course, if Dr. Peterson is an asshole, it's not going to matter of it's awesome, and that's got me worried."

Abraham sat up, incensed. Someone was messing with his woman. Every protective response in his body was on high fucking alert.

"He bounced my friend Linda out of the program already by cutting her TA hours and dumping them on me." Ani's eyes were bright with upset. "I wanted to give them back, but he wouldn't hear it. Linda really needed the money, so she took a part-time job, and then just couldn't keep up with the demands of the work and her proposal. I found out that she's quit the program. I couldn't talk her out of it."

"Somebody needs to talk to this guy." Abraham bristled. "This is bullshit. Can't you go over his head? Can't she?"

"If you're lucky, you could go to a dean or something... but the dean might not want to deal with it, either. especially if this is the sort of thing that has been happening for a while. Like, habitually."

Abraham gritted his teeth. "So they just let this shit ride?"

"It could be worse in the eyes of the administration, I hate to say." She sighed. "He could be plagiarizing. He could be keeping students back so they could do his dirty work, so he can maintain funding. He could be actively trying to fuck the female students. Instead, he's doing sneaky shit to fuck them over, because he thinks women are too hysterical, emotional and unreliable to be in a lab setting."

Abraham felt pissed. "I don't know anything about labs, but you are one of the most kick-ass, least hysterical women I've ever met," he said.

"You thought Tessa wasn't up to snuff..."

"Jesus, am I ever going to live that down?"

She stared at him for a long minute until he squirmed. "What?"

"You don't get to just brush off something because you feel uncomfortable," she said, her voice quiet but firm. "You were a jackass when it came to Tessa. You didn't believe in her. You were belittling. I don't care if you were that way with men too, you were insulting," she said, with her hand up. "So just because you feel differently about her now doesn't mean that you don't have to hear about it anymore now that you're friends with her or whatever."

"I just don't see why rubbing my nose in it is going to make anything better," he said, knowing full well he sounded surly. "How long am I supposed to pay for this?"

"That's the thing. I am not bringing this up to punish you or whatever. I was bringing it up to make a point, and you instantly made it about you."

He straightened, surprised. "What do you mean?"

"This guy is like you used to be. He doesn't think I can cut it. He thinks he's perfectly justified in doing what he's doing. And he thinks that, if he bounces me out, he's strengthening the program." She shrugged. "So you can say that it's shocking that they let this shit ride — but how long did they let Tessa stay moldering in audio?"

He blinked, trying to counter her logic. "Tessa never told anyone she wanted out," he said, but knew that wasn't true. She let Adam know immediately, as soon as one of their engineers left. "And she never put herself forward."

"Granted, she could've been more assertive. But she was doing quality work, and none of you paid attention to it," Ani said. "When she did put herself forward, as you say, you could've been more open to it, as well. The whole culture's messed up."

He frowned. He didn't want to admit that she had a point, but again: she was the least hysterical person he knew. And what she was saying made sense, as much as he hated that the thought.

"All I'm saying is, it's easy to say that my adviser's the problem, but the problem's just *there*, you know?"

Abraham felt disturbed. "So that's it? You just hope that he doesn't screw you over?"

"That's pretty much it," she said. "What would you do?"

Abraham grimaced. "Probably beat the shit out of him."

"I'll keep that option in reserve," she said, and kissed him.

CHAPTER 10

Ani straightened up, smoothing any wrinkles out of her clothes before going to Dr. Peterson's door. She'd been thinking about the conversation she'd had with Abraham all day. She was going to have her proposal defense in one week. Was she simply deluding herself? She'd been working so hard, both on his menial shit and her own work load. The proposal itself was golden, she knew that. But what if he torpedoed her?

Abraham was many things, but he was direct. Maybe she needed to be more direct. Maybe he'd respect her more if she was.

She knocked on the door.

"What?"

Not an auspicious start, she thought, as she entered. Then she walked inside. "Your calendar showed this was office hours, and you didn't have anyone waiting," she said, hating that her voice sounded so submissive. I hate taking up your time.

"What is it?" he said, his voice still displeased.

"I wanted to talk to you about my proposal defense."

His eyebrow went up. "Don't tell me. You need more time, and you want to push out the deadline." He sighed. "Why am I not shocked?"

His instant assumption slapped at her. "No! No," she continued, modulating her tone when both his eyebrows went up and his gaze bored into her. "I am ready. I've been working hard on it."

"Oh?" His voice held a note of skepticism. "So why are you in here?"

I want to find out if you're going to screw me over. Oh, why had she thought this was a good idea?

"I had some concerns," she said slowly.

"Concerns," he echoed, gesturing to a chair and leaning forward.

She wished she could stay standing — sitting across from him felt too much like a child being reprimanded — but she took the chair he'd motioned to. "I appreciate you making me your TA, but I hated taking the position from Linda, who was consequently no longer able to stay with the program."

He frowned. "I don't see what any of this has to do with your proposal defense, Miss Ani."

"Jeffrey has also been giving me the bulk of the grading," she said, plowing forward. "And I can't help but notice that of the experiments you've been assigning, over sixty percent of the lab work, plus about seventy to eighty percent of the cleaning and grunt work, has fallen on my shoulders."

There! She had statistics. She had hard facts. He couldn't refute that.

Instead, he leaned back, looking like a fucking Bond villain. "I'm sorry. I was under the impression that you were doing well with your proposal defense?"

"I am," she said, seeing the trap, but too late.

"So what difference does it make what percentage I assign you?" he said, and the metaphorical trap snapped shut. "You can obviously handle the work. Others can't, or I have other things for them to do. I would think you'd find that flattering, that you're trusted with this, even after the stupidity with the pipettes."

She gritted her teeth. "But..."

"Or is this an equity thing? An equality thing?" He huffed out an impatient breath. "You women want equity, but when you're treated as equals, you complain that you're being handled unfairly. There are times when some students will bear the brunt of the work. Especially students new to my program. They don't complain about it. And they get rewarded in time as new students come into the program."

Hazing, she thought. Institutionalized hazing. But at the same time, she'd bet her right arm that his "hazing" was focused almost entirely on women.

"And yet you seem to feel that you're being treated poorly," he said. "I must say, this doesn't reflect well on your ability to work with the team moving forward."

She felt a cold ball of ice in her stomach at his words.

"I promise, I will take all of this into account with the proposal defense," he said quietly. The threat was clearly present.

She nodded, then got to her feet. She just had to survive through the damned presentation, she thought, gritting her teeth. Then, she'd be able to get out from under his maniacal reign.

As she got up, he stopped her. "Miss Ani."

She turned. "Yes?"

He handed her a piece of paper. "I do need another task from you."

Frowning, she studied what he handed her. "Is this... what is this?"

"It's a dry-cleaning receipt," he said, as if she were an idiot. "I've got my own presentation in a few days."

She glanced at the address. "But — this isn't near here. This is the opposite direction from my place!"

He stared at her, derision and amusement in his expression in equal parts.

"Miss Ani," he drawled, "I don't remember asking if it was. It should be ready by tomorrow. Pick it up by tomorrow night, will you?"

·♥·♥·♥·♥·♥·

The next day, Abraham was feeling pissy when he drove to the now-familiar parking lot in Washington Sound University. He was carrying a bag full of Indian food — something he hadn't liked prior to getting with Ani, but which he was now enjoying — and also the reason he was pissy: a couple of suits and slacks. *Men's* suits and slacks, to be precise. Ani had called him in a panic and asked that he pick up the dry cleaning if he was going to be bringing food, which she damned well knew he would be. He thought the dry cleaning was for her, maybe for the proposal defense thing. When he saw that they were men's clothes... well, it did not put him in the best of moods.

Who the *fuck* was she picking up men's clothes for?

He knew that the stormy mood had to be playing across his face when he stalked into the TAs room, because the blonde goober, Jeffrey, immediately beat feet and got out of there. Guess it wasn't his clothes.

"I got your food, and your dry cleaning," he said, on a growl.

Ani sighed, getting up and taking both from him, hanging the dry cleaning on a hook from the back of the door and putting the food down on her desk. Then she threw her arms around him, hugging him tightly. "Thank you. I know that was a pain in the ass, and I want you to know I appreciate it." She kissed him.

He didn't want to be distracted, and God knew, her kisses could definitely be that. He kissed her one more time, soundly, just to keep his temper in check and because he was feeling possessive. "So whose clothes are those, Ani?" he said, his voice sharp.

Her eyes widened. "They're... wait. You're not jealous, are you?"

He growled. "Maybe."

"Oh for pity's.... no, I am *not* having you pick up my side piece's clothes!"

"I don't know. I'm your food delivery boy, who knows what I'll be a sap for?"

As soon as the words were out of his mouth, he knew they were a mistake. Her eyes narrowed, then she took a careful step back from him. "I don't ask you to bring me the food anymore, you know. I appreciate it, but nobody's got a gun to your head to treat me nicely."

"I know that," he said quickly.

"So don't throw attitude that I'm turning you into some 'sap' because you are supporting me, taking care of me."

He bit his tongue, feeling his blood boil. "You still haven't answered my question. Whose clothes are they?"

"They're..."

"Where is my suit?"

An older guy with close cut gray hair and a suit strode in like he owned the place, his face looking like he'd just sucked on a whole lemon. Or maybe he had a lemon shoved up his ass.

"Ani? Where is my.... oh, there it is." He grabbed the dry cleaning. "I was expecting it this afternoon."

"You didn't say when you needed it, and I didn't see any presentation on your calendar for a few days," Ani said.

Abraham blinked. Was this Ani? His Ani? Sounding so... so nervous? So fucking submissive?

Which had to make this that Peterson guy. her new adviser.

Yup. He was definitely a dick, just like she'd said.

The guy sniffed at the suit. "Why does this smell like food?" he growled. "Indian food, no less. Good God. That stuff reeks!"

Abraham bristled. "I picked them both up at the same time."

It was as if the guy hadn't even noticed Abraham in the room, or realized he was present or an *actual human being*, until that point. "Who are *you*?"

"He's..." Ani waffled, as if unsure.

Now that fucking chapped his hide. "I'm Ani's boyfriend," he said sharply. "I bring her food because she rarely has time to eat on the schedule she has to working for you. Tonight, she needed somebody to pick up dry cleaning. Your dry cleaning, apparently." He put all the censure and irritation he was feeling into every syllable.

The guy looked at him with evident shock. Then he looked at Ani.

"You've got a.... himbo?"

Abraham was starting to lunge forward before he realized what he was doing. Ani leaped between them, putting hands on his chest. "Dr. Peterson, that was inappropriate," she snapped.

"Oh, I was simply joking," he said. "You're lucky that you have a strong man who is willing to be so.... supportive," he said, even though amusement was laced through every word. "And helpful. You don't find men who are helpful around the house, willing to run errands and whatnot."

Abraham knew what Dr. Peterson was saying: that Abraham was some kind of house husband, some wimp beaten into submission by Ani and her needs.

If he'd wanted to beat some manners into Jeffrey, it was nothing compared to what he wanted to do to this motherfucker.

Dr. Peterson didn't stop there, tilting his head and surveying Abraham like he was some sort of lab specimen. "So, do you have a job outside of this as well, or does Miss Ani support you?"

He felt his pulse beating in his temple. A quick glance at Ani showed her eyes were imploring.

"I'm a computer programmer at a game company," he finally said. his voice sounding like ground glass.

"Really?" The disbelief in Dr. Peterson's voice was clear. "I don't waste my time on video games, but my grandchild seems to love them."

I could kill him, Abraham thought. One quick snap of his neck, and it'd be done.

Ani seemed to read his thought. "I'm sure the smell is just from my food here in the room," she said quickly. "Once you get out of the office, it'll all be fine."

"It had better be. I'd have to have to send your young man back because of it," he said. Then he grabbed the clothes and walked off with a smug expression.

"Just let him go," Ani said, wrapping herself around him and whispering against his neck. "Just let him walk away."

"Somebody needs to take that guy down a few rungs," Abraham snarled, feeling helpless. "Don't worry, I'm not gonna hit him. But Jesus, he's an asshole."

"Yes, he is," she said with a sigh. "But he's the asshole who has my career in his hands."

Abraham's blood boiled. With impotent fury, with the absolute helplessness and unfairness of the situation.

"Why are you just letting him treat you like this?" he finally asked.

She sighed. "We've talked about this…"

"But it still doesn't make any sense."

Her eyes snapped. "It's easy to say when you've never experienced anything like this," she said.

"I was in the damned army. I think I know what it's like to have to take orders I didn't like."

"Oh, and I suppose you were kicking the asses of your superior officers, then?" she shot back.

"This guy isn't your C.O.," Abraham replied. "Besides, he's not acting like your commanding officer. He's acting like he's your emperor. Like he's some little lab god!"

She sighed. "It's just another week," she said softly. "I can put up with anything for that long."

"If he lets you," Abraham said.

They were silent for a moment. Then she sighed. "I've got some grading to do, but I'd love to have you come over after. Or I can go to your place."

She was handing him an olive branch, he knew it. But he was feeling too shitty to reach for it right now.

"I think I'll be gaming with the guys tonight. Online," he clarified. "Give me a day or two to cool down, okay?"

He knew that was the wrong answer, too, when he saw her expression fall. But then she steeled herself. Ordinarily, he'd say she "manned up" but Ani was always utterly, supremely female.

"Do what you have to do," she said, her voice flat.

He remembered what she'd said, in his bed, just days before.

I think I'm falling in love with you.

He sighed, then kissed her forehead. "Just let me cool down," he repeated. "I'll be fine. I promise."

She nodded in response, letting out a huff of breath. Then she let him go, and he stalked off towards his truck.

· ♥ · ♥ · ♥ · ♥ · ♥ ·

Ani knew when Abraham left after the dry-cleaning fiasco, and said he'd be steering clear of the lab for a few days, that he was really, really pissed. She couldn't really blame him: Dr. Peterson pissed her off daily. But he didn't really need to put up with Dr. Peterson, the way she did. She appreciated the fact that he hadn't caused a scene or verbally gone to bat with her adviser. That would've been disastrous.

She bet that Abraham's Alpha-male-ness was insulted, as well. While she didn't feel the need for him to be in a pissing contest with her adviser, she did want to make sure Abraham was okay. She knew that Dr. Peterson's insults were barbed and unfounded. He was feeding into the lab's culture of toxic masculinity, and he was only reinforcing Abraham's experience of it, something that had no doubt been honed by the military and what she knew of his father's view of women and men and how each gender should supposedly act and interact.

Abraham was hurting now, and still trying to make sure he didn't take it out on her, which she appreciated. She wanted to make sure he was okay. That *they* were okay.

She had stopped over at Kyla's first, hanging out for a second with Kyla and her honey Jericho, while picking up something she'd ordered.

"Enjoy it," Kyla had said, with a wicked grin, handing her the bag.

"I hope to," she'd replied. God knew they both could use the stress relief, and she felt like it would be a throwback to when they first got together. She stopped at her apartment to get changed, then she drove over to Abraham's house, praying she didn't get pulled over. Her pulse beat frantically with excitement.

She knocked on the door. She was wearing a trench coat in the summer, and while it wasn't that hot at seventy degrees, there was no way it was cool enough for the coat. Being summer, it was still quite bright even though it was nine o'clock at night.

He'd get a good look at her: trench coat and heels, in what was close to broad daylight. It had to be obvious what she was there for.

When he opened the door, he was scowling. "Come in," he said, turning his back on her.

Her sultry smile faltered. Not the welcome she was hoping for, admittedly. "You all right?"

"Getting there." He groaned, going back to his video game. "I said I needed a few days, Ani."

"It's been a couple," she said, biting her lip. "I just thought I could help with your mood."

He blew out a breath. "You weren't kidding. Your adviser's a major dickhead."

She sighed. That had to have been preying on him all that time. But would he talk to her? No. Of course, she'd been too busy to talk, but still, he hadn't exactly picked up the phone. They'd need to work on their communication.

"Yes, he is a dickhead," she agreed. "You knew that. I knew that. I'm sorry he went after you, though. That wasn't fair."

"The only reason I didn't stomp the guy was because it'd hurt you."

She cleared her throat. "That, and it'd probably get you in jail," she pointed out. "You'd go to jail? For something that stupid?"

Apparently it was the wrong question to ask. "I'd just slap some sense into him. If he's pussy enough to press charges, I'd take them."

She felt her own temper simmer. "Why? Why do you have to prove things with violence?"

"Would you really mind if I fucked up that asshole?"

She thought about it. "Honestly...on one gross, vindictive level, no. He's a jerk, and I think there would be a certain level of satisfaction seeing him scared and hurt. But that's not reasonable. That doesn't make it right. I want to beat him at his own game, anyway."

"Well, I'm not exactly Mr. Fucking High Road," Abraham said. "I only backed down because of you. I swallowed pride because of you. I let that guy talk to me like a fucking *bitch* because of you."

She felt herself beginning to get annoyed. "And which is the problem?" she shot back. "That you were mistreated? Or that it was because of me?"

He pulled back, startled. "This isn't about you."

"Really? You said '*you*' three times in the last minute. So forgive me if I'm confused," she said, crossing her arms and feeling her body slither against the trench coat. Of all the times to try feeling sexy, this was just not happening.

He sighed, rubbing his hands over his face and through his hair, leaving it in a mess of copper tousles sticking up haphazardly, yet still in a sexy way. "I don't mean to be mad at you," he finally said. "I'm frustrated because… dammit, I feel like I'm changing."

"Relationships change people," she pointed out. "And that's what we're in. A relationship."

"I know that," he said. "Believe me. I guess I didn't realize what that meant."

She stiffened. "And you're regretting it?"

"No," he said. "Absolutely not. I'm just…"

It was as if he finally got a good look at her, because he stopped dead, his expression turning puzzled. "Wait a second. What are you wearing, anyway?"

She stood up, shrugging off the trench coat. "I hope you're not regretting the relationships," she said. "because I don't dress this way for just anybody."

It was the autumn warrior outfit. She was wearing strappy heels with the autumn leaf bikini. She pulled her hair out from the loose braid she'd confined it in, and walked up to him, pleased to see him struck dumb by her appearance.

"I think you're done with your game now," she breathed, gesturing to the screen, which he quickly (and gratifyingly) turned off. "I think I've got something better for you to play with."

"Holy shit," he breathed, taking her in.

She smiled. Then she reached into the trench coat pocket she'd tossed aside, pulling out the flexible leaf mask that matched her outfit.

"What happens at con stays at con, right?" she teased.

He was on his feet in a heartbeat. "Oh, yeah."

"Well, you big stranger," she said, her voice going husky, "maybe we can just blow some steam off, huh?"

He scooped her up in his arms, taking her towards the bedroom, then kissed the top of her head. "Nice job distracting me," he said… and suddenly she realized. He thought that's what she was doing.

Maybe it was.

But on some level — he was still upset. And she wondered what it would take for him to get over it. Or if he would.

CHAPTER 11

Abraham was at work, still in an ugly mood, and everyone was steering clear of him. It wasn't that he hadn't enjoyed the sex with Ani — God knows, he had, and then some. Together, the two of them were frickin' explosive. But afterward, he'd still felt... not exactly cheapened, but placated.

Frankly, he'd still felt like she had his balls in her purse after the stupid Dr. Peterson episode. He fucking hated that.

Now, he heard the guys rattling each other, mostly nudging Jose.

"You're still dating Chun Li?" Dennis asked Jose, in his usual obnoxious way.

"Her name's *Kelly*, remember?" Jose said, his tone sharp. "And yeah. We've been together a month and a half now, just about."

"Tell me you're at least hitting that shit," Dennis said, with a laugh.

There was a time when he would've said the same thing, just about. Now, he wondered if it always sounded quite that dickish.

"None of your business... but yeah." Jose let out a goofy smile. "Yeah, I am."

"Figures." Dennis rolled his eyes. "Don't tell me... you're in lurrrrrrve."

"How the fuck should I know? It's been six weeks," Jose said defensively. "I mean, I really like her. Like-like her. You know."

"You're in like with her," Dennis said. "What is this, high school? Am I right, Abraham?"

Abraham shrugged. "What are we, teenaged girls? I don't give a flying fuck about who's doing what as long as you're doing your job."

"Sounds like the boss hasn't been getting any," Jose joked, to get the pressure off himself, no doubt. "Thought you'd hooked up with that girl from Erotic City? The one with the metal mask?"

"I did," he said. "I am."

"What, did you lose her number?" Dennis said. Then he grinned. "Don't tell me you're in love, too!"

Abraham froze, unsure how to answer that.

I think I'm falling in love with you.

He hadn't said it back, but he'd been feeling the same thing. He wanted to, but not when he felt so raw and vulnerable. Especially when he was still pissed about the whole Dr. Peterson thing.

Taking his silence as a negative, Dennis pressed forward. "And you're not even getting any?" Dennis asked, sounding flabbergasted.

"Trust me, I'm still hitting it," Abraham grumbled.

"Then why are you so butthurt?"

"I don't have to explain a damned thing to you," he said. "She's fucking beast mode in bed, absolutely an animal. Yesterday, she wore a gold bikini made of leaves. She'll do whatever you want in bed. I've got no complaints."

The guys stared at him. he was rather surprised he'd shared quite that much, himself.

"So what's the problem?" Jose asked, genuinely puzzled.

Abraham growled.

"Don't tell me," Dennis said. "She's nuts. Crazy to hot factor, yeah?"

"She looked pretty hot," Jose agreed.

Fezza shook his head. "Or maybe she's pressing for a relationship too quickly?"

"That's not a problem," he said. "It's complicated. She's got a lot of shit she's going through right now, and I'm just dealing with it, okay?"

"She's trying to pussy whip you, huh?" Dennis said sagely. "Chicks. Always trying to domesticate you."

"Well, I'm through being fucking domesticated," Abraham said savagely.

"Nobody's asking you to be."

The voice was female. He looked up, shocked — only to see Ani there. She held a bag of chicken from his favorite fried chicken place. She was also wearing an expression of pure, unadulterated rage.

"I hadn't told anybody about the sex," she said. "Nice to see you're having an open discussion at your place of work."

He winced. These guys were his friends, but she was right: it was a dick move. "Ani..."

"Oh, snap. You're screwing Ani?" Fezza's eyes bulged like billiard balls. "Tessa will castrate you with a melon baller!"

"I'm not afraid of Tessa," Abraham shot back. "And that's not the point here. Ani, can we step outside...."

"Nice," Dennis said with a low whistle, not helping Abraham's case any.

She tossed the food on his desk, then headed out with quick steps. Abraham had to practically run to catch up with her. "Would you slow down, goddamn it!"

"I don't know that we have anything else to say," she said. "You said that we don't have a relationship. I've got too much shit, too much baggage. And you're through being domesticated," she said. "I'm not looking to domesticate you. You don't want to be in a relationship? You're the one who pushed for one. You want everything your way. You think it's unfair that you do what women have been doing for centuries — being the helpmate, being the one who actually gives the support and the shoulder, who bears the burden quietly. Too much for you? Fuck. Right. Off." Her eyes sparkled like obsidian. "I don't need you, Abraham Williams. We're done here."

He felt his stomach clench like a fist. "No, we're not."

"You don't get to say that. Do you understand?" She got in his face. "You don't get to be an Alpha-hole and then decide you're going to push until you get your way. I have enough to deal with, and I am through with *your* baggage. I am done with *you*, do you understand?"

He reached out, kissing her.

She pushed back, and then slapped him. Hard.

"*Done!*" she shouted, then went to her car, slamming the door.

He felt like he'd been run over when she drove away.

· ♥ · ♥ · ♥ · ♥ · ♥ ·

Ani sat sobbing at the bookstore. She could've gone to her apartment, but the thought of being surrounded by mess and her defense proposal notes was somehow even more depressing than her current state of woe, so she went to the only place she could think of to provide some kind of comfort.

Cressida was there, and Tessa was on her way. Hailey was out with Jake, and Rachel was still at school. She was waiting for Tessa to come home. Fortunately, there weren't many customers, and Cressida had ushered her back into the private area, the kitchen, so she wouldn't be disturbed. When the customer left, Cressida went back to her, giving her a hug.

"You okay?"

She liked Cressida. Cressida was always kind to her, always a good listener, and bottom line, utterly non-judgmental. In fits and starts, she told her everything about the adviser, about her relationship — or non-relationship, if what he said was true — with Abraham. By the time she was done, she was crying all over again. Cressida just listened, putting an arm around her shoulders, bringing tissues, and nodding.

"It sounds bad, doesn't it?" Ani said finally, when the storm of crying and anguish finally burst itself out. "I feel like an idiot. I should've just kept it physical: what happened at Con could've just stayed there. But I got greedy."

"Sounds like the sex was awesome, and he was actually being a good guy," Cressida said. "Now, keep in mind: I've got no practical experience myself. But it also sounds like he had the deck stacked against him. From what Tessa's told me, those guys are all 'guys' in the Tim Allen mode — growling, over-the-top, Alpha dog guys. She's lucky she got Adam, honestly. And I know what gamers are like," she said, with a dark tone. "Trust me, I've played enough MMO's to know what men can be like online. So that's the culture he's coming from."

"So that makes it all right?" Ani said, incensed.

"Absolutely not. I think you're right, the relationship's hosed there if he doesn't grow and learn," Cressida said, and Ani wiped at more tears. "But I think we can see where his attitude comes from. Sounds like his Dad was super-toxic-masculine, and he's surrounded by his sisters who are stay at home moms who went along with their father's idea of the gender status quo. And then he went to the military, and *then* went into games. The only way he could've gotten more toxic is if he'd gone to prison or something."

"I don't care," Ani said. "He doesn't get to treat me like shit."

"No, he doesn't," Cressida said fiercely. "He absolutely doesn't, no matter what the reason. He'll need to grovel like hell for any sort of chance... and even then, maybe he shouldn't get one."

"You're a good friend," she said, hugging Cressida again.

"Thanks." Cressida leaned back. "I'm more concerned about your adviser, anyway."

Ani felt her chest shrink, collapsing in on itself. "So am I. Oh, God, so am I. I don't know what I'm going to do there. I think he's going to hose me, and there isn't anything I can do about it."

"You walked away from Abraham, because he wasn't treating you right," Cressida pointed out.

"This is my future," Ani said. "This is my *life*."

"If it were all about love, you chose to walk way because it wouldn't be worth it," Cressida said, her voice low but persuasive. "Is it worth living your professional life in the shadow of all this? Is this the way you want the rest of your life to go?"

Ani sighed, gritting her teeth. She wanted to go into this to make a difference — to help save lives. What would happen if they didn't let her? What would happen if they told her that she would have to just do grunt work forever?

Would that make it worth it?

"No," she finally breathed. "No. It's not worth it."

"So you're gonna have to fight for it," Cressida said. "Trust me. I know what it's like to be afraid of something, like your life depended on it."

Ani felt a stab of guilt. "I feel badly. Here you are, fighting every day..."

"No, don't do that," Cressida said quickly. "I didn't mention that for you to feel sorry or feel 'inspired' or any of that. I just... I get it. I get how you're feeling. And if you decide to ride with it, I'll still support you. But I also get the feeling that you won't be happy, and ultimately that'll eat away at you," Cressida said. "Just think about it, okay?"

Tessa came in the door at that point. "How are you? Do I have to kill Abraham? Or your adviser? Anybody else?" Tessa's eyes glowed with vengeance.

Ani hugged Tessa, then hugged Cressida again. "You guys are the best, the absolute best," she said, wiping at her eyes. "I'd drink, but I've got proposal defense, and I can't afford to until that's done. But I think I've got a plan..."

· ♥ · ♥ · ♥ · ♥ · ♥ ·

Fortunately, none of the guys had given him any shit when he walked back into work after Ani left. If anything, they made themselves scarce for the rest of the day, no doubt because of the murderous look on his face. Apparently, he'd broken up with Ani — or, more to the point, she'd broken up with him, hard. He could still feel the slap, still heard her shout of "*Done!*" ringing in his ears.

He may well have fucked up, he realized a few days later. But she'd made it clear: she didn't want to hear anything else from him. She didn't want him making this about him, he thought with anger. So he was doing what she asked. Staying the hell away from her. Letting her tackle her proposal defense without him. Live her life without him.

Too bad it made him feel so damned awful. Breaking up with Becky had been a sort of relief. Breaking up with all his past girlfriends, even the long-term ones, had been varying shades of resignation and irritation. But this? This was like getting torn up with a rusty chainsaw. He drank heavily, by himself, playing video games until he passed out in his gaming chair. He'd gotten drunk enough to throw up, which he hadn't done in years. It hadn't helped his mood at all. Now he was stone cold sober, and he couldn't stop thinking about her, couldn't stop focusing on what he could've done differently — and how it all went wrong.

There was a knock on the door, and he frowned. Ani, his heart thought, jumping a little. He went to the door.

To his shock, there were his parents on his doorstep.

"Is everything all right?" he asked immediately. His father didn't like to leave the farmstead unless he absolutely had to, and his mother just went out for things like food shopping or hanging out with her church group.

"Sure. Your mother just wanted to go to some knitting store up here, and she wanted me to drive," his father said, with a shrug.

Abraham's eyes narrowed. He knew damned good and well that his mother drove everywhere by herself. "What is this, really?"

"Ah... your sister might've called you the other night, and said you were upset."

He winced. He should've known better. Should've shut off his phone when he got roaring drunk. "Which sister?"

"Darla." His mother sighed. "So, you're having some trouble with that girl of yours, are you?"

"I told your mother to stay out of this," his father said to Abraham, heading to the kitchen and helping himself to a beer. "But you know how she is. Just has to get involved."

His mother ignored that little comment. "What happened?" she asked instead.

He sighed. "I screwed up," he said. "I won't go into details, but I was getting upset, and I felt... I don't know. Resentful."

"Resentful why?"

In fits and spurts, he let out details: how he was bringing her food, making sure he was there for her, bringing her to get her equipment fixed... and then putting up with shit from her adviser being the straw that broke the camel's back. He noticed his father getting more and more incensed.

"You were absolutely right to dump her ass," his father ground out. "Jesus Christ. Does she want you to be absolute pussy? Hand you your balls in a Ziploc bag?"

"Carl!" his mother said sharply. "What was he supposed to do? Just.... just beat the man for being unprofessional and snide?"

"For being disrespectful!" his father roared. "And she expects you to just stand by while someone acts like you're some... some pussy househusband?"

His mother rolled her eyes in obvious frustration.

"Don't you roll your eyes at me, Helen!" Carl snapped.

Abraham jumped up. "Don't yell at Mom!" he snapped back.

His mother held up her hands, her voice trembling. "Boys, please."

Abraham's father scowled, but he nodded, and Abraham backed down a little, his heart beating fast. "Ani was right. I couldn't just beat up someone because he pissed me off. It didn't have anything to do with me, really. He was messing with her," Abraham said, realizing it for the first time. "The guy's got nothing to do with me."

"He was treating you with disrespect," his father disagreed. "You just gonna take that? You could've backed him down, put the fear of Abe into 'em..."

"Dad," Abraham interrupted, "it would've messed with her career."

"Oh, her *career*," his father said. "If her *career* is more important than you, then you're better off without her, anyway!"

He frowned, thinking of what she'd said. "If you had to give up being an electrician to be with Mom, would you?" he asked.

His father frowned back. "Why the hell would I have to give up that?"

"Just... would you? Would you have changed your career to be with her?"

"That's different and you know it," his father scoffed.

"You know how you make fun of my job all the time? Yeah, you do, Dad. You think I should still be in the army, and I've learned to deal with that," he said sharply when his father started to splutter his denial. "But the fact is, she could be saving thousands, maybe millions, of lives, if she does what she does. Her job *is* important. And even if it wasn't — if she loves doing it, why do I need to make her choose between letting me have my pride, and letting her have her career? What is that all about?"

"What the hell are you talking about?" his father said, obviously baffled. "You sound like one of those ... those feminists!"

Abraham shrugged, feeling exhausted. "I don't know what I sound like," he said. "But I know that I love this girl, and I hurt like hell not being with her."

"You're making your choice then," his father said, his eyes matching Abraham's, gray and icy. "But don't come crying to me when she leaves you like some... some wimpy loser!"

He stormed out.

"He's just angry," Abraham's mother said. "I'll calm him down, and we'll get through this."

"Mom," Abraham asked. "Why do you put up with all this?"

She sighed. "Because I love him," she said.

"Just because you love someone doesn't mean you have to put up with bullshit," Abraham said quietly.

She straightened. "I handle your father in my own way," she said, with soft but firm pride. "That said — I think you're right. You messed up with this girl, dear. Make it up to her. She seems special, and I'd hate for you to lose someone you obviously care about so much."

She hugged him, then scurried off after his father at a quick pace.

CHAPTER 12

The day of her proposal defense, Ani was wearing a dress. She'd considered wearing a pants suit, wanting to look as serious as a malaria outbreak. But Cressida, Rachel and Hailey had convinced her that she didn't have to sacrifice being traditionally feminine, or enjoying that side of herself, to prove a point that she was serious, not hysterical, not emotional. She liked the way the deep fuchsia dress hovered over her legs. She could tell from one look at Dr. Peterson that he was *not* amused by the dress she was wearing. She adjusted the cloisonné pin on the lapel of her scoop-neck dress and walked over to him.

"Do you really think that this... this *outfit*," he said, his voice irate, "is appropriate for a proposal defense?"

"It's a Nordstrom dress, and it's professional," she said. "It's got a bright color, but I think that it's more than appropriate."

He pulled her aside. "You're not going to pass, you know."

She blinked. He was saying it. "What?"

"Your thesis. Your proposal. It's not going through," he said. "I can guarantee that."

She gasped, shocked that what she'd suspected was finally, baldly being confirmed. "But the rest of the board..."

"Will listen to me," he ground out. "I am your adviser. And I rather thought you'd take the hint. You don't belong here."

"Why not?" she said, standing her ground. "I've done everything you've asked."

"And questioned me on it!" His nostrils flared.

"I've done the grading with no problems. Carried out your experiments flawlessly," she said, her own voice rising a bit.

"But you've been insolent and emotional," he said. "You wouldn't see Jeffrey giving me the attitude that you have displayed, Miss!"

"Have you given him eighty percent of the grading and grunt work?" she shot back.

"I didn't need to. He knows his place!"

"And what is that?" she asked, throwing care to the wind. "You say that I'm emotional. How is this not emotional? I think that you're making this decision because you don't like women in your laboratory!"

He grimaced. "All you women say that."

"Not helping your case any."

"I'm not sexist," he said, his voice a jagged edge. "It's not my fault you women can't step up to the mark."

"It is your fault that you're trying to deliberately make them fail," she said, her voice clear and angry. "It's your fault that you're deliberately telling me that, no matter what, I will not be able to pass. That you are going to torpedo my proposal defense because you feel like I don't belong in a lab."

"You won't be able to prove it," he said. "I don't need to explain why I don't feel you're ready yet. I am your adviser. I don't have to prove a god damned *thing*."

She smiled. Then she pulled the recorder out of her pocket. She rewound it, until his voice piped out. "Your proposal, it's not going through. I can guarantee that."

"That's... that's not legal!" he said. "I'll sue you!"

"Do that," she said. "In the meantime, I'm bringing this to the Dean, and to the board. This is sexual discrimination and harassment. And I have proof."

"I'll make sure your career is ruined," he said, his eyes bugging out like a pug's, his complexion red as a tomato. "I'll make sure you never get a job in any respectable laboratory anywhere. You might think you've won, but trust me — there are enough people out there, *men* out there, who still listen to me and who will know you set this up as a vendetta against me. Your career is *over*!"

She felt a momentary pang of terror. What if he was right? Was her career over before it had even begun?

She swallowed hard. Then nodded.

"So be it," she said. "I'm going to do this because it's not right — and because I'm not going to roll over and be scared of you, play ball because you might throw me some scraps. I deserve this, and more importantly — no other woman deserves to deal with your bullshit fear tactics. If it means I lose my career but I save a bunch of others, then I guess it's worth it."

· ♥ · ♥ · ♥ · ♥ · ♥ ·

Abraham didn't believe it was possible to miss one human being so much. She still hadn't contacted him, although he'd learned from Tessa that she'd stood up to her adviser and was now giving him hell – and it sounded like the rest of the advisory board was listening to her. He wanted to tell her he was proud of her. He wanted to hold her and congratulate her. He wanted to hold her, period.

But no, you had to go and be a jackass.

He knew that he'd have to grovel if he was going to make this right. And it couldn't just be a grand gesture, not flowers or chocolates or diamond jewelry or something. He needed to show her that he understood how exactly he'd fucked up... and that he wouldn't do it again.

It took some convincing to get the bookstore sisters, friends, and Tessa to get on board with him, but he finally won them over. Getting the guys from MPG to go to the bookstore wasn't a hardship, because... well, the Frost sisters were hot, and the guys didn't mind any opportunity to check them out and try and charm them. Granted, it never worked, but hope sprang eternal at Mysterious Pickles.

"When is she getting here?" Jose asked, his arm around his new girlfriend, Kelly. "I want to take Kelly to dinner at the Italian place, over on Railroad."

Abraham let out a low whistle. "Nice," he said. "I don't know when she's going to get here, but you don't have to stay."

"No, I want to," Jose said, smiling. "You're making a big move here. Believe me, I get how difficult it is to stand up to the guys, and stop being that douchebag when it comes to women. Once I met Kelly," and the look he gave her was gentle and joyous, "I knew I didn't want to be that guy anymore."

"Well, she may not want me, so wish me luck," Abraham said. He couldn't remember feeling this nervous before, ever. Not before football games, not when he was in Afghanistan, not before game launches. Possibly because Ani meant more to him than anything he'd ever experienced before.

He just had to let her know that.

"Hey guys," Ani's voice called out from the entryway. "Lot of cars tonight! Is there a sale..." Her words petered off as she got a look at the MPG guys – and then Abraham. "What are you doing here?"

The deep freeze of her voice was not promising, but Abraham girded himself. "I'm groveling," he said.

Her jaw dropped slightly. "You're what, now?"

"Groveling," he continued doggedly. "I fucked up. I know that now."

Her eyes narrowed, and her arms crossed. "Why should I even listen to you?"

"Because I'm learning."

"So you've changed."

"No. Not entirely," he said, wanting to be completely honest with her. "I am going to screw up more, I know it. And I am still going to have – what did you call them? – Alpha-hole tendencies. If we're together, I'm going to think of you as my woman. I'm going to want to protect you and provide for you and beat any guy who mistreats you to a bloody pulp."

She stared at him.

"But I'm also going to realize that you can take care of yourself. And that it's not all about me, and I need to stop trying to make it about me. I'm going to remember that taking care of you means listening and stuff like doing laundry and bringing you dinner or making you chai when you're hungover."

He saw it: the small smile. Hope bloomed in his chest like an atom bomb.

"And I'm groveling in front of not only your friends, but the guys from MPG, because I was an asshole when I was with them, and I want to show you that I'm not just saying this when it's easy. I'm not just acting one way in front of you and another in front of the gang. I don't want to be that guy."

"So, he's *begging* to be whipped, then? That's why we're here?" Dennis stage-whispered to Fezza.

Abraham sighed. "Specifically," he clarified, pointing at Dennis, "I don't want to be *that* guy."

Ani took a few steps forward, her arms still crossed. Her dark brown eyes were rimmed with tears. "You really hurt me," she said slowly. "It still hurts."

His arms ached to hold her. "I'm sorry," he said. "I'm so damned sorry. I never want to hurt you again."

She stared into his eyes. Then she sighed, nodded, and leaned forward. He eagerly folded her into his arms, feeling her arms weave around his chest.

"I missed you," she said. "And I'll forgive you. But if you hurt me like this again…"

"I can't promise I won't screw up on other things," he said. "But I won't hurt you like this again. That, I can and will promise."

"I'll work with you on it," she said. And kissed him.

EPILOGUE

2 Years Later

Ani was nervous. She stood in front of the full-length mirror in the bedroom, holding the robes she was going to wear shortly in front of her. In just a few hours, she was going to walk across the platform and receive her doctorate. Right now, she was dressed in a flame-to-peach colored dress that Kyla had made for her. Her parents were in town. Everyone from the bookstore was going to be there.

"You ready?" Abraham asked, sneaking up behind her and wrapping his arms around her waist, nibbling at her neck as he took in both of them in the mirror. His gray eyes glowed with approval. "You look amazing."

"You always say that. Even when I'm in sweats, you say that," she said, leaning back and nuzzling her head against his chest. "Not that I'm complaining."

"I always mean it," he said.

She'd moved in with him a year and a half ago, and she hadn't regretted it for a second. When he promised not to hurt her like that again, he meant it. He'd spent that time taking care of her, becoming more supportive than any spouse she'd seen in the program. He gave her back rubs, he made her food, he did the laundry.

Every now and then, he'd have gaming parties at the house. She'd hear "the guys" giving him shit about being a house husband. To her shock, he never rose to the bait. Instead, he'd remain chill with Adam and Rodney and Jose, and shake his head.

"You guys don't know," he said, looking particularly pitying when it came to Dennis. "Someday you will."

Now, he was kissing her, holding her. She wished there was a little more time before they had to get to the campus, so she could show him in a much more physical way just how much all his help and support meant to her.

"I couldn't be here, couldn't have done all this, without your help," she said, her voice clogging with emotion.

He shook his head. "You're one of the strongest women I know. And they got rid of that asshole Dr. Peterson, so you got to work with Dr. Kantor. You would've made it regardless."

"Everybody who does something like this needs help. I had you. I want you to know that I never want to take you for granted," she said. "You said you'd never hurt me, and with whatever stupid fights we've had, you've kept your word."

His eyes were shining, and he turned her to face him, kissing her gently.

"I love you," he said.

"I love you back," she said, kissing him a little harder. "I'm glad we're celebrating with everyone tonight, but I swear, tonight, you're going to get a special show. Just you and me."

"Oh?" His eyebrow went up.

"This dress," she said, gesturing down, "isn't the only thing I had Kyla whip up for me."

"*Oh.*" His smile was fierce. "In that case – I can't wait for tonight."

She was still laughing when he held her hand. "I've got something you can wear in the meantime, though. I didn't have Kyla make it, but I hope you like it anyway."

She paused, puzzled, when he reached into his pocket and pulled out a small velvet box. Her heart caught in her chest.

"Is that...?"

"Will you marry me, baby?" he asked, and his voice actually shook. "Because I don't want to be without you. Ever."

"Yes," she said without hesitation. "Yes, yes, yes."

With that, she kissed him.

"That's my girl," he said, slipping the diamond on her finger. She watched as it flashed on her finger, catching the light like his eyes. "Anything you want, I want to give to you."

She pulled back to look at him, smirking.

"Think you can wear the leather pants and mask tonight?"

His grin was slow and broad.

"Oh… I think that can be arranged."

· ♥ · ♥ · ♥ · ♥ · ♥ ·

Thank you for reading Ani and Abraham's book! The next book in the Fandom Hearts series is Mallory and Simon's story. Ever wonder why Simon is so skittish in Snoqualmie? He and Mal have a past... and hopefully, a future! Check out **Ms. Behave**, *a Fandom Hearts novella.*

A Note From Cathy

Thank you so much for reading *What Happens at Con.* The Fandom Hearts series is all about finding the things you're passionate about — the things you're *geeky* about — and going all in. I loved writing this series, and I hope you enjoy reading it just as much. The series is complete (I think? For now? Although some of those secondary characters *have* been nudging at me!) and each book can be read as a stand-alone, although they can be enjoyed in chronological series order for the full experience. And there are other series to enjoy if you're looking for more fun, geeky love stories!

If you do enjoy the book, please take a minute to write a review of this on Amazon and Goodreads. Reviews make a huge difference in an author being discovered in book searches and shared with other readers!

And if you'd like to connect with me, I love hearing from readers! You can stop by www.CathyYardley.com to email me, or visit me on social media. Or join my Facebook readers group, *Can't Yardley Wait,* to see early reveals, exclusive content, and a lot of shenanigans with a very fun group.

Enjoy!

Cathy

ABOUT AUTHOR

Cathy Yardley writes fun, geeky, and diverse characters who believe that underdogs can make good and sometimes being a little wrong is just right.

She likes writing about quirky, crazy adventures, because she's had plenty of her own: she had her own army in the Society of Creative Anachronism; she's spent a New Year's on a 3-day solitary vision quest in the Mojave Desert; she had VIP access to the Viper Room in Los Angeles.

Now, she spends her time writing in the wilds of Eastern Washington, trying to prevent her son from learning the truth of any of said adventures, and riding herd on her two dogs (and one husband.)

Want to make sure you never miss a release? For news about future titles, sneak peeks, and other fun stuff, please sign up for Cathy's newsletter here.

Let's Get Social

Hang out in Cathy's Facebook group, Can't Yardley Wait

Talk to Cathy on Twitter

See silly stuff from Cathy's life on Instagram

Never miss a release! Follow on Amazon

Don't miss a sale — follow on BookBub

ALSO BY

THE PONTO BEACH REUNION SERIES

Love, Comment Subscribe

Gouda Friends

Ex Appeal

THE FANDOM HEART SERIES

Level Up

Hooked

One True Pairing

Game of Hearts

What Happens at Con

Ms. Behave

Playing Doctor

Ship of Fools
SMARTYPANTS ROMANCE

Prose Before Bros
STAND ALONE TITLES

The Surfer Solution

Guilty Pleasures

Jack & Jilted

Baby, It's Cold Outside